MW00882617

A forest with no trees

Peter Hey

This book is a work of fiction. Names, characters, places and incidents are either products of the author's imagination or used fictitiously. Any resemblance to actual persons, living or dead, businesses, companies or events is entirely coincidental.

© Peter Hey 2015   1.1.1

ISBN-13: 978-1517461614
ISBN-10: 1517461618

All rights reserved, including the right to reproduce this book or portions thereof in any form whatsoever.

For Clara, whoever you were.
And for my Clara. You know who you are.

Oh, and for Burnley. I've grown to love you. Honest.

Prologue

I don't remember yesterday.

It's a lie, of course. What I mean is, I remember so very little. Most of it is lost, like a feature-length film cut down to a handful of frames. All I'm left with is a series of brief highlights: visual snapshots, extracts of conversation, vague suggestions of emotion. If you ask me to try hard, really hard, I can expand those snippets into longer passages, but is it recall or extrapolation? Fact or assumption? And those passages, if I add them all together, what do I have? Twenty, thirty minutes? Certainly not a day. The balance has been edited out and discarded by an aging brain, tired of repetition and desperate for space in its cluttered, grey filing cabinet of finite and failing neurons and synapses.

And what of last week, last year, my entire childhood? The further back I go, the sparser it becomes. Whole years seemingly blank, interspersed with the occasional high or low, sometimes with meaningless banalities. Certain events burnt into my memory forever amidst an empty wilderness of lost time. I'm left with a series of images, things I've witnessed and done. But how many pictures are in my album? How many episodes in my drama? Surely a few thousand at most. Some of them, I know, lie hidden, only to be exposed when triggered, by a smell, a sound, some random prompt. Others trick me: false memories, often reinforced by years of confusion and self-deception. A half-remembered sentence becomes a chapter. Another person's story becomes my own.

And when I die? The electricity in my brain stops pulsing; the chemical messages stop flowing. Are my memories immediately wiped like the blackboard at the end of a lesson? Or do they rot slowly as my tissue is eaten away beneath the ground, or burn to ash and smoke in the fire of the incinerator?

And then? The significant find their place in histories; those of us more mortal may leave the scantest of trails, suggestions of a life: the odd photograph, officialdom's record of birth, marriage and death. Is that to be my only trace, just chemicals on card, coded pixels on a hard drive, a few lines in a file or database? If my descendants look into my face in years to come, who will they see?

Chapter one

'My name is Tom Haworth and I fear nothing.'

It was a July day with a November sky. He stood alone on the empty hilltop and shouted his oath onto a hard Pennine wind. This was the maxim that would guide him through life. He would face every challenge and run from no-one and no thing. He was eighteen.

The King's English had seemed appropriate for a solemn vow, but he saw the contradiction and repeated the words in a more honest language.

'Me name's Tom 'aworth an' ah fear nowt.'

He paused and winced at the memory of a wooden ruler cracking down over his knuckles. 'Not even Miss Ashworth.' Then, smiling to himself, 'Not anymore, anyway'.

His old schoolmistress would not tolerate slang and dialect in her presence. 'It will label you as a common man, a common woman' she would insist, despite knowing that was her pupils' lot in life. There would be no doctors or lawyers amongst them; they were all fodder for the mill or the mine or the farm. It was six years since he'd escaped the tyranny of the village classroom, and his teacher's clarity in correcting that which displeased her had made an indelible mark. But it was only a mark, not a scar.

At this moment, Tom felt anything but common. He was a skilled man; he had status and respect amongst his peers and he had the heart to move on, to seek something better. His future was bright and it lay before him now, picked out by a hard-edged shaft of sunlight slanting through the heavy clouds.

He had climbed the rounded summit of Thwaite Pike. Behind him barren slopes led down towards his home in the valley of Blackwell Brook. Ahead of him, far below but illuminated like the object of some holy quest, lay a vast urban sprawl. They said 100,000 people lived there; they were indistinguishable at this distance, but he could make out the long railway viaduct and row upon row of stone-built terraced houses squeezed between squat mills whose chimneys formed a smoking forest against the skyline. Single-storey weaving sheds spread out low and wide, their sawtooth-ridged roofs catching the light in sharp stripes like the furrows of freshly ploughed fields. Tom knew that under those roofs lay tens of thousands of looms producing mile after mile of cotton cloth destined for every corner of the Empire and beyond.

Miss Ashworth ensured her pupils understood their birthright. Britain and its benevolent Empire spread justice and progress throughout the world. There was no doubt, no question. Britain's greatness was founded on industry and the county of Lancashire was at its heart. To be a Lancastrian, common or otherwise, was to share that greatness.

The clouds closed together and the great town lost its ethereal glow, returning to grey-grime industrial gloom. For Tom, however, the spell could not be broken and the optimistic smile remained on his face. For a man such as himself there were opportunities in those darkening mills.

But he wasn't going to go on his own; there was someone he had to take with him.

The wind cut mercilessly through the jacket he'd happily carried over his arm down in the valley. A downpour threatened, with occasional mists of fine drizzle blowing through and reddening his face. The moors of the Rossendale Forest could be bleak, even at the height of summer. The rolling uplands were covered with coarse grass, moss and clumps of rush; no tree could survive the harsh, acidic soil. Here on the western reaches of the Pennines, the prevailing winds blew clouds up and over the hills, and the resulting rains fed springs and fast flowing streams, which cut sharp-sided cloughs into the landscape. Man had left other mysterious scars: long-abandoned quarries and shallow mines, disguised by the weathering of time and nature's return. An ancient packhorse trail wound its way across the high ground avoiding the boggy hollows, centuries of foot and hoof carving it deep into the landscape. A distant, solitary farmstead, Scout Top, braved the heights and a wide, irregular lattice of dry stone walls fanned out, keeping a few hardy sheep from straying too far.

This stark beauty had brought Tom up onto the moors, but the wind and cold conspired to send him down. With the strength of a young man, the climb had taken him most of an hour; the descent would be only a little faster.

Soon yellow-brown scrubby grass and rush gave way to greener slopes. Flocks of sheep and a few cows kept the pasture short, and a handful of farm houses were spread out at a respectful distance from one to the next. But this was no rural idyll.

Ahead and below, Tom could see Spring Mill. Approaching from its north side, he could make out the characteristic rows of skylights set into its zigzag roof. The spinning mills of Manchester could soar to eight glass-walled storeys, but the heavy vibration of the looms used for weaving required them to be fixed on solid ground, in expansive low sheds lit from above.

In the middle distance lay three more tall square chimneys rising from the other mills that employed most of the local villagers. Some of the men toiled at Habb Colliery, a small pit sited halfway up the valley side; from its entrance a long diagonal tramway carried coal down to a grubby depot on the road below.

When he reached the valley floor, Tom walked up a pathway separating two short rows of terraced cottages. Nearly all construction in the village was in locally quarried stone, but only the very newest buildings showed its natural colours: honey yellow and golden creams. After a few years everything became blackened by the ever-present smoke and soot.

Tom knocked on the door of the third house on the left. A woman, who looked older than she probably was, opened it and smiled.

'Tom. You alright lad?'

'Aye, Mrs Lord, I'm grand. Just been up t'tops. Is your Bill about?'

Mrs Lord turned and shouted for her son, who soon took her place at the door.

'You coming down t'Towneley?' asked Tom.

'In't it a bit early?'

'I've been up t'tops and I've got a thirst on.'

'You've always got a thirst on. Hang about, I'll get me jacket.'

Fifteen minutes later they were standing in the taproom of the Towneley Arms and Tom was ordering their second pint. Their mothers allowed them a few shillings from their weekly pay, and most of it went over this bar. The shillings allowed to their fathers tended to be spent in the Commercial Inn, the other village pub which was the haunt of the older men.

'You've got no clack, Tom' said Bill, acknowledging his pal's renowned capacity for downing beer as if he had no throat or 'clack' in the dialect despised by Miss Ashworth.

They were born in houses a few yards apart, went to school together and now worked in the same mill. Bill was, by common consent, the finest looking boy in the village. Tom's features were more robust, but he still attracted admiring glances from the girls in the weaving shed.

'How you getting on with Ann then?' probed Tom.

'Ann's being very friendly, very...' Bill paused while he searched for the right word and then smirked when one with an impressive number of syllables came to mind, '...very accommodating.'

'Two cees, two emms' he added to prove he could spell it as well.

'Good for you,' said Tom in admiration. 'I'm sure Miss Ashworth would be proud of you. I'm not sure about Ann's dad, mind. You gonna wed her then? Can you cope with her mithering and that temper of hers?'

Ann Pilling was beautiful. She had strong, rounded features, cascades of black curly hair, dark chocolate-brown eyes and dimples in her cheeks when she smiled. Her figure filled out her dress like a tightly bound bale of cotton. All the boys wanted her, but she came with a price. Ann was notoriously vain, moody and spoilt. At school she was always the slowest in class, but also the loudest. She mocked the plainer, brighter girls and toyed with the boys. But those boys always came back for more.

As he took a mouthful from his glass, Tom felt a little jealousy, partly from carnal desire but also because Ann Pilling was a trophy. To have Ann on your arm granted status, and that was something that mattered.

'How about you. How's it going with Clara?' asked Bill.

Clara was one of the plainer, brighter girls Ann had mocked in class. But Clara had a kindness that matched her intelligence. She was mousy haired but slim and tall, and from the right angle and in the right light, almost pretty. Catch her from the side and her beaked nose jarred slightly, but even that could grow on you in time. And it had grown on Tom. He knew that if Ann was the trophy, Clara was the real prize.

'I made up me mind today. On t'moors. I'm leaving this backwater and going to Burnley. Clara's coming with me as me wife. I haven't told her yet, but she knows it's what I want.'

It was not in Tom's character to think she might say no.

Chapter two

'My name is Tom Haworth and I fear…everything?'

He looked at his face in the bathroom mirror. The downlighter directly above emphasised the hollow cheeks and the black grooves under his eyes. He looked old. The grey flecks in his thinning sandy hair confirmed the diagnosis: old and very, very tired.

He knew he didn't really fear everything. He didn't fear spiders or dogs. He didn't fear thunderstorms and he didn't fear dentists or their needles. All the things his mother told him not to be afraid of. But what about the people around him? What about life itself? She hadn't mentioned those.

Tom hadn't had a drink for exactly six months, a major milestone. He might have expected a sense of achievement, victory even, but there was none. His psychiatrist recognised that an underlying depression had led to his dependency and prescribed a course of Cognitive Behavioural Therapy and antidepressants. But the CBT had seemed aimed at someone else's issues and the pills did nothing to lift his mood. They were little more than placebos; the Internet said as much. All that stuff about synapses and blocking serotonin in the brain was bollocks. He still felt down. He still felt scared; he just wasn't sure what of. The doctor had switched him to something new, but that did nothing too.

At least he had something to feel depressed about these days. His wife had finally left him when the drinking had got out of control, and there was no way he was going to keep the job in the bank when he stank of booze every afternoon. And then there was that expensive mistake when he couldn't think straight. They would never have him back, and he hadn't the confidence now to look for a decent job somewhere else. That's how he ended up working for the Mills.

Chapter three

On the day of rest, Tom's mother allowed him a lie-in until 7:30 am. Shaken from a heavy sleep, his throbbing head immediately reminded him of the night before. The usual gang had made it to the Towneley and gallons of beer were drunk until the landlord, George Tattersall, decided he'd had enough and turfed them out just after midnight. Tom's detailed recollection of the evening was patchy but it came back to him as the morning progressed, piece by piece, like the picture emerging in a jigsaw puzzle. He'd held court as usual. The boy who was captain of the school football team still retained that status as a man. It helped that, at 5' 11", he was a head taller than most of them. Only 'Lanky Harry' outstripped him now, but Harry's vertical growth seemed to have sucked muscle and flesh from his feeble, bony frame. In contrast, Tom was what his mother called 'right strapping'. On their occasional forays into the nearby towns of Bacup and Rawtenstall, the village boys would sometimes fall foul of local lads, and Tom could always be relied upon to look after his pals and bust the odd nose if necessary. It was part of their Saturday evening entertainment, and the spirit of the Marquess of Queensbury ensured no-one was ever seriously hurt.

Today there were no scrapes on his knuckles and the only damage he felt was self-inflicted and chemical. But young men recover quickly. After breakfast he donned his Sunday best and prepared to go to church with his parents and his two younger sisters. The five of them shared a four room terraced house. If it was cramped, none of them noticed. It was certainly a world away from the two rooms in which his father's family of ten had been raised. There was more space now Ethelina had married and moved out. Little Sarah Alice had also left them, but a different church service had marked her departure. If Letitia Haworth still felt the loss, she kept it to herself. It was a grief she shared with many of the other mothers, and she was not a woman to show weakness.

The sun shone warmly this Lord's Day, and the sisters chattered and giggled as they made the short walk to the Baptist church. The building sat in the narrow valley, facing the road and spanning the Blackwell Brook on stone arches. The small graveyard at its side had quickly filled, so the congregation had purchased some additional land occupying the flat top of an adjacent spur looking down over the church roof. A steep path climbed diagonally up the wooded slope between the old burial ground and the new.

Tom's father hushed his daughters with a stern look and led them up the incline to pay their respects to their sister. The grey-black stones underfoot were dry, but he silently remembered how treacherous they had been on that foul day he had borne her little coffin on his shoulder. George Haworth was Victorian. He did not cry at her funeral, but of all his children, she was the one to whom he'd found himself showing affection. Naturally taciturn and partially deaf from a boiler explosion in his youth, he seldom spoke more than a few words with the others. Their upbringing had been the responsibility of his wife; he knew their characters were reflections of her, not him.

Tom lingered behind as he saw Clara arriving with her parents and brother. When she noticed Tom she smiled and opened her eyes wide as a greeting. He nodded in response and watched them walk into the church.

The minister, Percy Franklin Chambers, was an educated young man from Warwickshire. He had a melodic, soft Midlands accent but enunciated his words very clearly in case they were lost on ears tuned to broader syllables. He was not a man prone to tub-thumping, but one thing that would put fire in his words was the evil that was drink. Like many nonconformists, he was a champion of the temperance movement and on a mission to convince his flock to follow his teetotal example by signing the pledge and renouncing alcohol for good. Clara and her family had taken the oath with enthusiasm, but many of the other faces in the pews looked at the floor guiltily whenever the minister's sermons hit upon their most recurrent theme.

After the service, Tom sought out Clara and asked if she would take a walk with him up to the reservoir. She agreed and along the way they chatted happily about the local gossip. Tom's was sourced mainly in the Towneley Arms, but he skimmed over the previous night so as to avoid her disapproval. When they reached the earth dam the conversation faltered, and Tom wondered if it was the right time to discuss the decision he had made the previous day. Before he could assemble the right words, he saw the expression on her face darken.

'Have you read the papers?' she asked.

'I was never one for reading much. You know that, lass. You were always the clever one in class, always picked things up first. You won Miss Ashworth's handwriting prize year after year.'

'Don't put yourself down, Tom. You were always good at arithmetic. A head for figures you. Anyway, the Manchester Guardian thinks we really could go to war over this business with the Austrian archduke. The one who was shot.'

Tom tried to look concerned. 'Who's going to be fighting who?'

'Britain, France, Germany, Russia, they could all get drawn in. I don't really understand, but things have been building up over the last couple of weeks. The archduke was assassinated by a Servian. If Austria declares war on

Servia, the Russian Tsar will declare war on Austria, and then the German Kaiser will declare war on Russia. France and, to an extent, Britain have alliances with Russia so they might have to go to war with Germany too. The Guardian's dead against us getting involved, but it sounds like events are getting out of control. Some people are already starting to wave flags and bang drums. Oh, Tom, if the great empires of Europe start fighting, so many men will be killed. It will be awful!'

Tom smiled reassuringly. 'I'm not sure we've any business getting involved in a war over Servia. I'm not that certain where Servia is, but we'll be fine. Britain's the most powerful country on the planet. We'll give Germany a damn good hiding.'

Clara looked at him earnestly. 'The Royal Navy might rule the waves, but compared to the Germans, and the Russians and the French, our army is tiny.'

Tom took her hand and looked straight into her mid-brown eyes. He wanted to say that, for her, he'd fight the Kaiser, or the Tsar, and all their men. He hesitated because he knew it would sound silly and crass: armies were made up of proper soldiers, not millworkers.

'It all sounds a long way away. I'm sure it won't affect us, lass. Everything here will stay the same, trust me' was the best he could muster.

Chapter four

Tom Haworth had worked for six years in Forest Mill, a short walk from his home. His father was a foreman overseeing the throstles which spun the cotton thread, but Tom was a weaver.

The contraptions on the spinning floors sang like the birds that gave them their name, but walking into the weaving shed for the first time was like entering a vast, deafening mechanical hell. Its demons were 240 iron-bodied power looms the size of bedsteads and crammed together in 8 lines of 30. Rotating, grinding steel shafts ran overhead for the entire length of the room, and from them flapping leather belts looped down to drive the gears and cranks of each machine. As they did so, metal arms threw 240 sharp-nosed shuttles clacking from side to side and 240 frames clattered up, down, back and forth, lifting warp threads open and closed and beating the weft down into the emergent cloth. Each loom repeated the cycle three times every second and together they made the floor vibrate and hum. It was possible to find a rhythm in the cacophony, but it was unceasing and all-enveloping. The bodies moving carefully between the cogs and picks of the unguarded machines breathed humid air thick with dust and fibres. Any conversation was limited and only possible through exaggerated lip movements and facial contortion.

Tom was a skilled man. He could now run six looms at once, tending to their demands and turning miles of thread into yards of grey-white cloth. It was piecework: the more he produced the more he got paid. He was also spending time with George Ormerod to learn the ropes as a 'tackler': a man who supervised up to 100 looms and their weavers, and tackled any mechanical problems and adjustments. Tom was certain weaving was the future. The great town of Burnley did little else and its countless chimneys beckoned him with limitless prospects. But for today he worked alongside people he had known all his life.

The early mills had been built in high river valleys, where fast flowing streams provided the driving force for the first machinery. The development of steam power meant that larger, more profitable mills could be built in flatter lowland areas, and industrial towns had sprung up all around Lancashire. The county had a damp climate that suited the cotton fibres, and its extensive coal fields fed the engines and boilers. As well as mills, the towns had engineering works building the heavy, complex machines that spewed out thread and cloth. An extensive network of railways soon developed to replace canals as the main arteries of commerce and linked the towns to the market centre of Manchester and the port of Liverpool.

The high moorland valley of Blackwell Brook had been home to some of the early mills producing woollen cloth. They clung to water power for longer than most but eventually gave in to the inevitability of steam. Woollen production had then largely been phased out in favour of cotton. Space was tight along the narrow valley floor, but a ribbon of small mills and hamlets grew to stretch from the head of the valley down three miles to where the Blackwell flowed into the River Irwell. Even at the height of railway mania, no engineer was mad enough to consider driving a line up the Blackwell valley, so its mills still relied on horse wagons to feed them raw materials and take away finished yarn and cloth. Ultimately, the mills were only viable because of the supply of local coal. If they struggled to compete with the larger town mills, such was the demand for King Cotton that their owners still made handsome profits in the boom years of the late 19th and early 20th centuries.

It was early evening on the first Tuesday in August 1914. Tom had been helping to replace a damaged crank arm and was delayed leaving the weaving shed. There was still warm, hazy sunlight when he entered the street and began his journey home. A small crowd had gathered in the narrow lane to the side of the Commercial Inn and it drew Tom towards it. Bill Lord was next to Ann Pilling, and Tom went to stand behind them. He looked over their shoulders to see a large man looming threateningly over a smaller figure half lying, half sitting on the dusty ground.

Jim Bradshaw farmed up at Scout Top. He was squat, heavy and thick-necked; his face was blasted red by a lifetime on the high moor. When sober he was notoriously charmless; when drunk he became paranoid and violent.

On the floor was Frank Hindle, 17 years old, slightly built, round shouldered and sallow. He was shaking with fear as the farmer slurred and spat at him to stand up and take what was coming to him.

Bill half turned and said quietly to Tom, 'Jim's been in the Commercial all afternoon. Had a skinful. God knows what Frank's done to rile him. You know how the lad scurries round everywhere. He'd have been on his way home from work. Maybe he just ran into Jim when he staggered out of the pub.'

'Well, I think spindly Frank Spindle probably deserves it. Serves him right for being clumsy and gormless' chipped in Ann. There was an obvious relish in her voice.

Bill ignored her. 'We going to try and stop this, Tom?'

Tom shook his head slowly. 'It's not my fight' he replied.

Frank had always been shy and awkward at school. Some said he was a bit 'simple'. Tom, for one, had always looked down on him. Only Clara made any effort at friendship. At the mill, Frank made faltering attempts at fitting in with the other boys and men, but whilst never deliberately ostracised, he was quietly ignored. He came in; he worked his machine; he went home.

'He really looks up to you, Tom' suggested Bill.

Tom stared at Frank pitifully cowering on the ground but felt scant compassion. He warmed to the kindness in Clara's character but valued only strength in his own. He had always suspected his coldness was inherited from his father.

Even so, he found himself speaking out across the crowd. 'That's enough, Jim. Go home and sleep it off.'

Tom's words were not calming and conciliatory but were loaded with threat and aggression. He still didn't care about Frank; he was doing this for himself. He had something to prove.

He stepped past Bill and gestured that his friend stay back. He strode to within four feet of Jim Bradshaw and stopped.

'I said, that's enough. Go home and sleep it off.'

Tom felt a tense excitement. His nostrils flared and the hairs bristled on the fists clenched at his side. He had taken a vow to be afraid of no-one and no thing. In life you had to face your enemies, call them out. So what if you risked a beating? The alternative was to run away, and once you started running, you would never stop. Now was the time to show himself that he meant it.

And, if he'd been honest, it always helped if your enemies were so drunk they could barely stand.

Jim Bradshaw swayed slightly as he turned to size up his young challenger. Ten years ago he knew he could have beaten him down easily, ground his face into the dirt. But those ten years had been hard: relentless toil, remorseless weather and ruinous drinking. He felt a faded likeness of the proud man who once saw himself as the king of the high moors. Alcoholic melancholia swept over an already wretched soul, and he just wanted to stagger back to his run-down farmhouse and bolt the door. He just wanted to sleep.

Facing Tom, he raised a shovel-like hand and pointed a bloated finger. His face formed into a menacing grimace, but there was only tiredness in his eyes. The face sank. The arm dropped. He mumbled something incomprehensible and then turned and started to walk away, shuffling unsteadily down the lane.

A wiser, calmer man would have let him go quietly, but Tom was high on adrenaline and triumph. 'Yeh, crawl off, you fat begger.'

Jim Bradshaw stopped. The small crowd held their breath.

The heavy-set farmer stood still and, heavily and deliberately, pulled air through his nose like an angry bull. Nonetheless, the swaying, floating sensation in his head refused to steady. He couldn't clear his thoughts. All he knew was that he was as drunk as he had ever been, and it was over. Any vestiges of pride and self-respect had collapsed, like a neglected barn roof when the damp and rot have finally taken hold.

After a long pause, his head dropped lower and he simply continued on his way.

Elsewhere in Europe that day, the Schlieffen Plan to attack France via neutral Belgium was being activated by the Kaiser's general staff. Belgium had refused the ultimatum to let troops cross its border, and Britain had promised armed support to the smaller country should she be attacked. The Germans came anyway.

Chapter five

Jimmy Mills was a barrow boy and proud of it. Barrow boy was the standard derogatory term for working class men who made good in the banks and businesses of London, supposedly behaving like they were selling dodgy goods off a barrow in some backstreet market. In reality, their middle class counterparts, the successful ones at least, had very similar ethics; it was only the accents that differed. Jimmy's father had 'made a bob or two' running a popular country pub, but Jimmy played up his lowly origins. He was the poor boy made good, and everyone was greeted with a cheery, 'Alright, mate?' His Essex charm could sell anything to anyone, and he liked the expensive things in life, expensive and ostentatious. His new Range Rover had the full Premiership footballer options pack, and his wife's Mercedes sports car was barely more subtle. For Jimmy there was no point having money unless you flaunted it for everyone to see.

He had always worked for himself and now funded his lifestyle through a lucrative business training bus drivers. Jimmy had never driven a double-decker in his life, but London bus companies had a high turnover of staff, and EU regulations insisted on regular training without being too specific on what it should encompass. That created a niche teaching vocational topics such as health and safety, customer care, and disability awareness to compliment more practical driving and road skills. A handy EU grant helped with funding and JMS Bus Training was the acknowledged leader in the marketplace. (JMS originally stood for Jimmy Mills' Skills, but had quickly been initialised).

Jimmy's wife looked after staffing and recruitment, and she tended to hire staff in her husband's image. The ability to joke and blather your way convincingly through a thin syllabus, ideally in a Estuary English, was the primary qualification. She had been surprised, therefore, when her husband told her to give the nod to the nervous middle-aged man with the flat northern vowels.

Tom Haworth had worked in the City in the back office of a small international bank. With his statistics degree he'd been recruited into the risk management department. Careful and conscientious, he was valued by his employers but what was seen as a lack of drive meant he was passed over for promotion. As support staff, the back office were treated with some contempt by the high-earning front office bankers, and their demands sometimes put stresses on Tom that he struggled to deal with. The money was good, if not great, but his lawyer wife started to leave him behind financially. Work pressure intensified after the financial crash; his drinking got out of hand, and his neatly organised life began to fall apart. Amanda decided she'd be better off on her own; all their friends turned out to be her friends, and finally he lost his job. Any confidence he had left went with it.

He managed to get control over the drinking, but Amanda, whilst happy being estranged, felt she had to step in to get him working again. She was a business acquaintance of Jimmy Mills and called in a favour. Tom was desperate. He'd had some training responsibilities at the bank so felt, if anything, overqualified for this poorly paid job in a dingy office in a grubby part of south London. Tom didn't know if Amanda just felt guilty or actually still cared about his welfare, but he had been grateful. He was less grateful when he found out she'd had an affair with Jimmy. A prouder man would have resigned on the spot, but Tom had no pride left. He sometimes thought about telling his smug employer's smug wife about her husband's infidelity, but Jimmy looked like a man who could turn nasty, and Tom really did need his job. And besides, Carol Mills had always treated him fairly; she idolised her husband, and Tom didn't want to hurt her simply out of spite.

Despite his misgivings, Tom took his work seriously. He tried his best to understand the full ramifications of what he was teaching and to think up real-world examples that would help his students, many of whom didn't have English as their first language and often looked lost and bored.

If he didn't fit in well with his fellow instructors, Tom was popular with the young girls who ran the office. He always had the time and patience to help them with accounts and figures, and was an absolute wizard when it came to spreadsheets.

On one course he shared training duties with Carl Singleton, a squat, ugly man with an aggressively shaven head and a background in the motor trade. Carl would brag about conning people into buying clapped-out cars or spending hundreds of pounds on unnecessary repairs. 'Gift of the gab, mate. He who blags, wins.' He would happily blag his way through the training sessions, inventing dubious explanations or skimming over those sections he didn't fully understand. 'To be fair, you don't really need to know this bit' was one of his favoured expressions.

One hot afternoon, towards the end of what had felt like a long, difficult course where several of the attendees had struggled to follow the material, Carl was talking about an EU regulation and totally misrepresented what it was trying to achieve. Tom made the mistake of gently correcting him in front of a class. Carl laughed it off at the time but cornered Tom once the students had left for the evening.

'What do you think you're playing at? You think you're so clever with your fucking university degree. But don't you ever make me look small again, you fucking wanker!

He jabbed a stubby finger into Tom's shoulder as he stood within inches of his face. 'I know what you are, you geek. You're just a fucking pisshead! A sad drunk.'

Tom could feel spittle on his cheeks as the words were spat at him like venom. He could also taste the fried lunch on Carl's breath and smell the stale sweat coming from his sticking, yellowing shirt as the vitriol continued.

'You think you're better than me, but we all laugh at you behind your back. All this stuff we teach, it's crap. A tick in some pointless EU box. You're the only one who don't see it. You fucking wanker!'

Carl Singleton had lifted himself onto his toes to look Tom in the eye. He now dropped down and the fiery redness in his face began to recede. 'Just keep out of my way. Understand?'

He made an exaggerated gesture of pulling back his shoulders and audibly sniffed. 'Wanker' he mumbled and then turned and swaggered out of the room.

Chapter six

There was a gap in the training schedules and Tom decided he had to have a break. His holiday year was nearing its end, and if he didn't use his entitlement soon, he was in danger of losing it. He hadn't been sleeping well and now his encounter with Carl had unnerved him. But as he told himself, it could have got much uglier had he responded to the abuse. They were only words, after all.

On a whim he decided to go home to Burnley. He still called it home but he hadn't lived there for twenty-five years, and there was no-one there for him to go back to anymore. His sister lived abroad and his mother and father had died some years back. It had to be six years since he'd visited the town, and even then, he and Amanda had passed through on the way to somewhere else. She'd always hated the place.

He no longer had a car so made his way across London to Euston Station. He hadn't done the trip by train since he was a student. Back then, it had been a regular journey at the start and end of every term. This time he'd bought the tickets online, but without booking much in advance, the price of his 'off-peak' return had made him wince. He was sure it was much cheaper back in the flat-fare days of British Rail, when you just turned up, bought a ticket and got on the next train.

The cavernous 1960s' concrete box that formed the station concourse was more cluttered than he remembered. His father would talk fondly of the original Victorian ticket hall and the famous arch, but this was Tom's Euston. It symbolised home and a connection with the past.

He was early so grabbed a quick coffee before making his way down the ramp to the gloomy, almost subterranean platforms. The train looked sleek and modern, and it seemed to stretch on forever. It was a long walk before he reached coach U and climbed aboard. He found his allocated place next to the window and apologised to the pretty young girl in the aisle seat who had to stand to let him past. She was wearing earphones and looked at him blankly as he squeezed in and sat down.

The train left on schedule and glided smoothly and almost noiselessly into the sunlight and along the broad track bed that cut through north London, tall walls of blue-black engineering brick funnelling the line through modern tower blocks and smart Victorian terraces. It was some time before the urban landscape gave way to countryside. Tom couldn't concentrate on the paperback he'd brought to pass the time and found himself idly staring out of the window. He was wary of falling asleep as he could wake up in Scotland if he missed his stop. Roads, fields, villages and towns passed by, and some of them at least, looked very familiar. Certain clear images, the remains of a Norman castle and strange churchyard mounds feet from the track, came back to him from the recesses of his mind. How many times had he travelled on this line, seen these things fly past, wondered where they were, and then forgotten them? But they weren't forgotten, they were dormant in his deeper, long-term memory, just waiting for a stimulus to bubble them to the surface years later. And they brought with them the feelings of the younger man who last saw them, full of optimism and strength. He was briefly transported to a happier time, like the smell of candy floss taking you back to childhood holidays. He held the mood for a while, but then it faded. Though he could still bring the pictures to mind, the emotions were lost to him.

He left the Glasgow train at Preston. The station was still unmistakably Victorian, though cleaner and brighter than he recalled. The ironwork supporting the long station canopies had been painted white, with the finer details picked out in red and green. There'd been a short delay outside Crewe, but he managed to make his connection and boarded the stopping train to Burnley Central with three minutes to spare. He was carrying only a small case so had been able to dash quickly across the ornate footbridge between platforms.

As the scruffy, two-carriage diesel pulled noisily out of the station in the direction he'd just arrived from, an even more familiar landscape began to fill the windows. Even so, tiredness finally caught up him and he felt himself dozing as he leant his head against the side of the carriage. He was jolted awake when the train stopped at Blackburn but quickly drifted off again. He was more relaxed about missing his station. Even if he did sleep through, the line only carried on for a short distance. Despite avoiding the early swings of Dr Beeching's axe, the track to Yorkshire and beyond had been lifted in the 1970s.

He awoke to find the train stationary. It sat on an embankment across the end of a short, narrow street with terraced houses either side. Once identical, the frontages of most of the homes had been painted. Generally they were similar shades of cream or off-white, but one stood out in a slightly flaking powder-blue. Only two of the houses retained their original bare stone walls; both were blackened by time, but one homeowner had picked out the lines of mortar in white. Up and down the street, the front doors were a variety of colours and designs, and the effect was like two neat ranks of soldiers wearing a jumble of uniforms. There were cars parked along one side of the street, and only two people were visible: a young boy of six or seven, holding a football, and a woman who leant down over him with her hand on his shoulder.

Tom's eyes closed again and when they re-opened the scene had changed. It was another short, narrow street. The design of the terraces was the same, but everything seemed fresh and new. None of the walls were painted, and the doors and windows seemed to match. There were no cars and the road had an unmade dirt surface with no pavements. Wisps of smoke from some unseen fire hung in the air. Another boy was talking to another woman. The woman wore a long dress and her hair was tied up in a bun. The boy looked dishevelled and his clothes were grubby, like he'd been rolling on the ground. His shirt tail was hanging out of his shorts.

Despite the fixed train windows, Tom could hear the woman's words clearly.

'You'll have a right black eye in the morning. And this shirt will take me ages to sew back up. I don't know what you'll wear to school tomorrow.'

'He started it, mum.'

'He's twice your size, just wait till I see his mother.' The woman took her son's shoulders in her outstretched hands, straightened him up and looked him squarely in the eye. 'But you did right. Never does any good running away. You did right. I'm proud of you.'

The train jolted into motion again. Tom blinked sleepily and the row of terrace houses slipped past. In another instant he was fully awake.

He was struck by how vivid the dream had been - he could still smell the smoke in the air and see the faded colour of the woman's blouse - but it was obvious to him what had prompted it. He knew he'd been running away from things for most of his adult life. He might have expected the woman to look like his own mother but she didn't. She was someone else. Maybe that was the point, if you could say there was any point to the wanderings of your subconscious mind.

Soon they were rattling along again at what passed for full speed and entering the outskirts of Burnley.

Looking down from the tall viaduct that dominated the town centre, he saw a mixture of old and new, but the overall impression was one of emptiness. Derelict mills and tired terraces had been swept aside, and a once cramped townscape now seemed to be nothing more than a succession of car parks fronting characterless buildings. News reports had politicians claiming that Burnley's economy was 'booming' after years of contraction, but the station and its surrounds suggested otherwise. Tom wondered if he'd just been spoilt by years of living in the affluent South

The cotton industry's slow demise had begun after the First World War. There was an attempt at resurgence in the 1950s, but during the 60s and 70s mills were closing across Lancashire at a rate of almost one a week. A handful lingered on until the 80s, when foreign competition finally silenced the last of looms. Tom's father witnessed much of the decline but had won a scholarship to Burnley Grammar School and escaped the shuttles and the bobbins for the security of a job behind a town hall desk. Tom enjoyed a relatively comfortable upbringing, and in turn, found his own escape through university. Like most of his contemporaries, he left Burnley behind him as soon as he could.

Tom exited the station and walked the half mile or so to the cheap guesthouse he'd found on the web. It was close to his old home and reasonably central. Mrs Hindle answered the door and after a few pleasantries showed him to his room. It was comfortable and clean though the furnishings were somewhat feminine. If there was a Mr Hindle, he'd had no say on the decor.

Denise, as she insisted on being called, was an attractive, if overly made-up, woman in her early sixties.

'Breakfast's at eight. Is that OK, love, or would you like it earlier? I don't know if you've got work to get to? There's only you and Mr Jones staying at the moment and he asked for it at eight, but obviously you can have it when you want. Within reason, of course.'

'Eight's fine thank you,' replied Tom. 'I'm here on holiday.'

'In Burnley? That's novel, I prefer the Canaries myself. Blackpool at a push.'

'I grew up here. I just fancied looking round some old haunts.'

'Most of my old haunts have been bulldozed, love. My mum and dad wouldn't recognise the place, rest their souls.'

Tom smiled. 'It's changed a lot since I was growing up, I must admit.'

He freshened up quickly but it was early evening by the time Tom left the guest house. He walked down mostly familiar streets until he found his old home. The house looked much the same apart from the ugly UPVC window frames and the peeling paint on the gate. A few scraps of litter had blown into the tiny front garden. It seemed like they might have been there some time. He continued on to the site of his old comprehensive school, which had changed its name and become a 'community college', before relocating to a £20 million '21st century learning environment' two miles away. The concrete and glass 1960s blocks of Tom's youth still stood and looked unchanged. Although empty, they seemed to have been preserved as if waiting for a new life. He briefly wondered if he would have been happier staying in Burnley as a maths teacher like his father had wished, but Tom quickly dismissed the thought. He had no time for regrets and what-ifs. For a man who worried and procrastinated over every decision, he had an oddly fatalistic acceptance of life's outcomes.

Retracing his steps back into the town centre, he realised he hadn't eaten since the pre-packed sandwich he'd bought on the train. Wandering around the main shopping area, all the cafés he found were closed. Then, briefly confused by the revised street layout behind the Market Hall, he stumbled on the Veevers.

It claimed to be the Hop Inn, but the original name, Veevers Arms, could still be made out in areas of slightly paler colouration on the jet-washed stone facade. Even without the ghost letters, Tom knew where he was. It was the pub where he and and his friends had first sneaked a beer at the age of 15. Looking back, their age was obvious, but because they didn't want to attract attention, they would always drink moderately and behave themselves. Tom wondered if it was really so much worse than the current generation of kids drinking themselves silly on cheap vodka and alcopops in some bus shelter or on a park bench. Obviously alcohol had eventually got the better of Tom but it was going to do that anyway.

The Hop Inn offered 'great food' until 9 pm. Tom hadn't been in a pub for 6 months but suddenly he was very hungry. He was also drawn by warm memories of evenings with childhood friends, when drink only made him laugh and smile. He told himself it was the next stage in his recovery; he would go in a pub and resist temptation. He would eat and have a soft drink. Part of him knew he was lying, but he had been caught unprepared. The emotional, impulsive side of his brain had taken charge, leaving his rational side wrong-footed and hesitant.

The bar was half empty. Most of the clientele were men on their own, though sitting around a table there was a small group which included a solitary woman. The interior had been remodelled since Tom's day, but even so, it had been a long time since a paintbrush had touched the woodwork or walls. The ceiling still had a noticeable yellow tint from years of cigarette smoke prior to the ban. A blue-topped pool table inadequately occupied the space once filled by the solid old snooker table that had been there for decades. Tom cringed in embarrassment remembering his 15 year-old self scoring a solitary red against an unamused older regular who'd been hoping for a proper game.

There was a folded cardboard menu at the bar. Tom scanned it briefly and without much thought decided on a burger. His mind was somewhere in the past. He ordered the burger, and whilst a voice in his head said 'Coke', the words that left his lips were 'and a pint of Moorhouse's please.'

He stood at the bar and watched as the barmaid poured the red-brown beer into a tall straight glass and placed it in front of him. It seemed to glow in the setting sunlight seeping through the frosted glass windows. He lifted it to his lips and took a deep swig. Conflicting feelings of relief and self-loathing swirled inside his head. It was as if he were being reunited with an old lover who had deceived him and caused him great pain. But she was so unbearably beautiful that he was compelled to take her back, knowing all the time she was laughing and would betray him again.

It doesn't take long to microwave a burger, but he was on his third pint by the time the food arrived. He ate it quickly and without enjoyment, and then switched to the double scotches. His money seemed to be going much farther than in his old pub in London. He was slightly bleary going to the bar for his second whisky when he noticed a man sitting in a far corner of the pub.

Tom didn't know why he hadn't seen him before. He stood out from the other drinkers. He didn't belong. He didn't belong at all.

He wasn't a young man, though he looked several years younger than Tom. He had a hairstyle that some of the trendy Premiership footballers seemed to be wearing, closely clipped around the lower part of the head but left longer on top and slicked back with some kind of gel or wax. Tom hadn't thought about it before, but it was really just the Brylcreemed 'short back and sides' of his childhood. Despite the haircut, the man's clothes looked unfashionable: fawn trousers, a plain white collared shirt and a red v-necked sweater. Whilst not having David Beckham's dress sense (or, presumably, budget), the man in the red sweater was strikingly good-looking. His jet-black hair had a defined wave despite the unction holding it down, and his dark eyes were set in a strong featured face. He smiled at Tom and slight dimples appeared in his cheeks.

Compared to the rest of the pub, the corner was in shadow and Tom's eyes struggled to provide sharp focus. He knew he must be mistaken. Even so, he considered walking straight out of the door. Then he realised he had no choice; he had to go over to the table.

'May I sit down?' Tom asked.

'Of course.'

The man had a packet of twenty cigarettes in his left hand; he had taken one out and held it like a pencil as he tapped the end, unlit, against the face of the pack.

The familiar but long-forgotten gesture dispelled any doubts in Tom's mind. 'You're not allowed to smoke in here, you know' he observed, distractedly.

The man's eyebrows furrowed, but he nodded in acknowledgement and put the cigarette back in the packet before saying, 'Look, I'd offer to buy you a refill but I'm not sure it's a good idea.'

'No, it's not a good idea, but I need one anyway. Can I get you one?'

Tom went to the bar, bought two whiskies and then took them back to the table.

The man gave a half smile in thanks before posing a question, 'How long was it since you last had a drink?'

'Six months.' Tom took a sip. 'Trouble is, you have one and you have to have another. I know that better than anyone.' He raised the glass to his mouth again. 'This place caught me off-guard somehow. I guess I'll just need a couple more tonight and then maybe I can start again tomorrow.'

'Start again?'

'Back on the wagon. Abstinence. Sobriety.'

The man looked doubtful. 'Until the next time?'

'You're supposed to learn from your mistakes. Hopefully this has taught me a lesson that will help me in the long term. What's the saying? "That which does not kill me makes me stronger."'

'There's an optimist in you after all, Tom.'

'He's in there somewhere, but he's pretty much lost most of the time. That's me all over, really. Lost most of the time.'

Tom paused, drank once more and decided he had to change the subject. 'I apologise. I'm getting all miserable, self-absorbed. A classic maudlin drunk. You look... I don't know... you look well.' As he said them he felt exasperation at the inadequacy of his words.

'Thank you. I'm not sure you do, but it is good to see you again.'

'Look, why are you here? What is this?' blurted out Tom.

'I feel I let you down. I blame myself. I wanted to see you, and for what it's worth, apologise.'

Tom looked at the man he had once idolised and felt guilty. 'Nah, it's not your fault. We choose our own paths. I just needed to be stronger, somehow.'

'But where do we get our strength from? I think mine came from my father.'

'Nature or nurture?' asked Tom.

'Who's to say? Both I suppose.'

'Look' said Tom. 'I'm going to be fine. Things are going to get better for me. This is just a temporary setback. Please don't worry.'

The man in the red sweater leant forward. 'A while back you said you were lost? Lost where?'

Tom sighed. He found himself repeating words he'd first used in the psychiatrist's chair. 'I sometimes feel like I'm wandering around in a thick, dark forest. Trees block my way everywhere I turn. I can't see the way out; I just go round and round in circles. But when I look closely, there's nothing there. No trees. The only barriers are in my head. As I said, I just need to be stronger.'

Tom's glass was nearly empty. 'Can I get you another?' he asked despite knowing that the other man's drink had hardly been touched.

'No thank you. I'm afraid I have to go now. I don't suppose I can convince you to leave too? It would be for the best, you know that. Come on, Tom. Put the glass down and walk out the door. While you're still sober enough to make the decision.'

Tom looked down at the table and shook his head. By the time he looked up, the man in the red sweater was gone. Tom knew he needed that drink more than ever.

The bell for last orders rang at a traditional 10:45 pm, and Tom felt some relief that his session had reached a forced end. Though he would never have any recollection of the journey, an unerring homing instinct took him back to his guesthouse and bed.

Chapter seven

He opened his eyes. He was outside and was sat upright against some kind of wall. He was stiff and his feet were cold and damp. Then he noticed the smell. It was familiar and yet like nothing he had smelled before. It was open latrines, rotting flesh, sodden mud and lice-ridden men who hadn't washed for a month. It was foul. It was nauseating. And it was normal.

There was an intermittent clatter coming from somewhere. It was a loud, banging rattle that sometimes echoed back, softer and more distant. Tom felt the urge to stand and look over the wall to identify the source, but instead he slumped down lower and pulled his tin hat forward so it sat squarely on the centre of his head. As he did so, something whistled through the air just inches above him.

He was tired. He felt like a man who had been awake all night and had just grabbed a few minutes sleep, hunched up and uncomfortable. He looked around him. He was sat in a small hollow cut into the side of what looked like a muddy ditch. There were rough wooden boards propping up the walls and running along the floor, where they were partly submerged in oily brown water. The ditch seemed to be haphazard and uneven, and a few yards either side of Tom it turned sharply back on itself.

Tom was not alone. One man knelt on a step carved into the opposite wall. He was peering through some kind of elongated box that reached over the rim of the ditch. The other men visible sat on the same step, either smoking, cleaning kit or staring distantly at the open strip of sky above.

Tom looked around and was overwhelmed by confusion. He knew each of these men. He knew their names and the names of their wives and children. He knew who they cried out for in their sleep. He knew which ones would fight, those who'd risk their life to drag you out of a shell hole, and those who'd freeze, the poor fools who'd stumble into the barbed wire, blind with fear, waiting to be cut in two by the arc of a Bosche machine gun.

And yet he also knew he shouldn't be here. He should be lying under the sheets in a pastel pink bedroom in Mrs Hindle's Burnley guest house, nursing a deserved hangover and trying to piece together the night before.

It was obviously a dark dream. Since adolescence he'd always been able to wake himself up in nightmares, as if his capacity for fear was lower than his threshold for sleep. But he hadn't woken up; he was still there in that hellish, putrid trench. He felt the tangible, physical exhaustion of a man who hadn't slept properly for days and whose nerves were taut in anticipation of a surprise attack or a well-aimed shell.

And then he understood. The mud, the smells, the damp, the sounds, the fear – they were all vivid and palpable. The other life, the guest house, the train journey, the strange job, the drinking - they were all vague and distant. That nonsense in the pub. That was the dream. He was awake now. This was reality.

He was Corporal Thomas Haworth of the East Lancashire regiment. He and his battalion were halfway through another stint on the front line. The previous night's patrol to repair the wire in No Man's Land had returned without casualties, but it had been a close run thing. The early morning 'stand to' was over; there had been no dawn raid to repel. The 'morning hate', the ritual of firing small arms and machine guns blindly into the mist, had relieved some tension, and bayonets were no longer fixed. Men cleaned their weapons in shifts while some were allowed a few minutes sleep. Sporadic shooting and distant explosions went ignored, but death and pain were always waiting over the lip of the trench or ready to come falling down out of the sky. Four more days, four more sleepless nights and they'd be rotated back to the relative safety of the reserve trench. In the meantime, Tom had to hold himself together and keep his men occupied. Inactivity bred boredom and boredom bred fear.

He looked across the trench. Bill Lord sat carefully slotting cartridges into the magazine of his Lee Enfield. His blonde hair had been cropped close to his skull and his face looked gaunt and drawn. He had an ugly red rash on his neck. He would no longer qualify as the finest looking boy in any village, not that he would care. Like his pals around him, all he cared about was staying alive and staying as near to warm and dry as he could. And of course, he cared about Ann. The one thing that kept him going was the creased photograph that was seldom far from his hand. It captured her dark eyes, her black curly hair, her curves and those dimples as she smiled up at him, telling him to keep safe and come back to her. In truth, their relationship had often been strained, but that was not something he ever chose to see when looking at her beautiful face.

In Tom's mind a clear image formed of himself and Bill walking over the hills to the recruiting office in Rawtenstall, two foolish young men with dreams of being heroes. They were posted to the same regiment and crossed to France still side by side. Since then, the only time they had been separated was when Tom took a shell fragment in his leg and had to spend four weeks in the Base Hospital. Apart from a few scratches, Bill had so far survived unscathed.

Bill had married Ann Pilling weeks after the outbreak of war. Everyone thought the conflict would soon be over and the valleys of the Rossendale Forest would remain untouched. Bill and Ann assumed they would never be separated, every night spent under the same roof, just like their parents.

Tom had not married Clara. She had been struck down by Rheumatic Fever, and for a time, the Hargreaves had worried that their precious daughter might be lost to them. She rallied, but her recovery was slow and she was confined to bed for several months. Even when she was well enough to return to the mill, the doctor warned against the more strenuous tasks as the disease had weakened her heart. By then Tom was in France, but before he left she promised to wait for him. It was the image of Clara's face that kept him going during the quiet, nervous times, and it was Clara he cried out for in his sleep.

Bill pushed the magazine into his rifle with a forceful snap. The man next to him visibly twitched.

Tom had a reputation as a hard man, a tough, uncompromising NCO who would shout and bully his section into line. But it was a kinder Tom who spoke to the jittery soldier, sat with his boots ankle deep in claggy mud.

'How are you finding your first time in the front line, Langport? It was a bit touch and go when that star shell lit up the sky last night.'

The young man still seemed to be shaking. His eyes were fixed on the floor and his reply was almost inaudible, 'It's fine, Corp. The lads have told me we've got it easy. It gets much rougher than this.'

'That's the spirit, Alfie' said Bill.

Tom's eyes met his friend's and then he looked back at Alfie. The other men had rough stubble on their chins. Alfie's was hairless, though red raw from teenage acne.

'Just remember to do what you're told, son. Look out for your pals but keep your head down and stick close to

Bill; he seems to lead a charmed life. We'll soon be back in the reserve trench. And then…' Tom paused. 'And then, none of us will think the worse of you. Write to your mum. Get her to send your birth certificate to the War Office. Demand they send you home.'

'I'm of age, Corp.' The reply was automatic and without conviction.

'None of us will think the worse of you. We're all praying for a Blighty ourselves.'

A 'Blighty', a wound just serious enough to render a man unfit for military service and a ticket back home, to Blighty. Tom had seen enough mutilated men to know such wounds would likely cripple you for life, but sometimes it seemed anything was better than this. Maybe he'd feel different when his nerves settled away from the front line.

There was a dull, hollow thud in the near distance, like a heavy rock plunging into water without splashing. A brief silence and then the sound became a whistle that seemed to be coming straight towards them.

'Mortar!' screamed Tom though every man already knew. Tom backed into the hollow in the trench wall, others ran towards the cover of a crude dug-out.

The trench mortar had a steep trajectory designed to drop high explosive shells straight down into enemy positions. When it came the loud explosion was just feet from where Tom cowered. The blast showered him in mud and stones and he felt a sharp pain in his shoulder.

It took him several moments to regain awareness. Ears ringing and still dizzy, he climbed down and into the trench, which was now shattered and wrecked. Earth was piled everywhere. An upturned steel helmet lay next to a khaki covered arm, perfect white hand at one end, nothing but sickeningly damp shredded fabric at the other. Where Alfred Langport had been there was just a single boot, standing vertically on the ground. The boot oozed red.

Tom looked away and saw another man lying against the wall of the trench. He was shaking and whimpering. His body was twisted and there was a bloody smear where his legs should be. His exposed stomach seemed to writhe unnaturally. Tom knelt down next to him. The face was blackened and burnt.

'He didn't move. I tried to grab him', spluttered Bill.

'Try not to talk.'

'Tom. I'm in a mess. I'm in a God-awful mess. Look at me. Oh Christ, look at me! You're my best pal. Please shoot me. Please. For the love of God, shoot me!'

Bill coughed and blood bubbled from his mouth. 'It hurts, Tom. I can't bear it. I can't bear to be like this. Please.'

Tom saw a rifle lying in the mud next to him but made no move towards it. 'I'm sorry, Bill. I'm sorry' he whispered weakly.

'What are you afraid of? Shoot me, Tom. Please, shoot me!'

For the first time since he was a child, Tom's eyes welled with tears. He knew his friend was right. He was afraid. When that pack horse had been torn apart by a shell, he'd put it out of its misery without thinking but now he was prepared to let his friend die a lingering, agonised, undignified death. He didn't know what he was afraid of: God, a court martial or just his conscience. But it was surely fear that kept his finger from the trigger.

Bill was reduced to sobbing and moaning, and Tom just knelt, hunched over, impotent and lost. He became vaguely aware of a commotion around him, the shouting of an officer, and then bearers arrived and pulled what was left of Bill, screaming, onto their stretcher.

Blood from the wound in his shoulder had soaked Tom's sleeve and was starting to drip from his fingers. He was told to follow the stretcher bearers back to the Regimental Aid Post. He had little recollection of the following hours but eventually found himself in a

Casualty Clearing Station, being discharged with his arm in a sling. He didn't know what had happened to Bill but was sure he was beyond medical help and by now, Tom hoped to God, had found the release he'd begged for.

Tom was several miles behind the lines with orders to make his way back to his Battalion HQ. Though it would cost him his stripes, he walked instead to the ruined farmhouse where they were billeted when away from the trenches. He found the hidden bottle of brandy he'd bought in Amiens and drank himself into unconsciousness.

Chapter eight

Tom's head ached and the roof of his mouth felt tacky against his tongue as if it had a coating of half-dry paint. He remembered lying down under a rough blanket, but this wasn't a farmhouse floor. He now found himself in a soft, comfortable bed. He didn't itch; he didn't stink. He opened his eyes. Light filtered through drawn curtains. He saw pink walls.

It took him nearly a minute to orientate himself and realise he was in his small room in Mrs Hindle's guest house.

He closed his eyes again, and the previous day came back to him in a series of sharp images. Their horror caused him to pull his knees to his chest as if adopting a foetal position could somehow take him back to a state of newborn innocence, newborn ignorance.

What was happening to him?

On one of the first dates with his wife they'd gone to see a horror film. One particular scene had unnerved them both and made them leave prematurely. It showed the lead character, a young American, having an horrific, graphic nightmare, but then he woke in a hospital bed. The film's background music softened to create a mood of calm and relief. The audience were fooled into relaxing. On screen, a pretty nurse came in, talked to the American for a while, and then opened the curtains. One of the monsters from the dream immediately leapt out from the window and brutally killed her. The young man woke for a second time, screaming, and the same nurse walked in again, unharmed. It had been a dream within a dream.

Was that what was going on in Tom's mind? What was nightmare and what was reality?

He opened his eyes. The walls were still pink. He felt for his shoulder. No sling, no pain, no wound.

Despite the scenes from the trenches seeming compelling and true, so, now, did Tom's life in London. He thought of his spreadsheets, of the Internet. Surely that was beyond imagination?

He looked at the digital clock by the bed. It was 7:40. He assumed it was morning. He wasn't sure when he'd last eaten and thought food might help ease his hangover. Maybe with a clear head things would start to make sense.

He got washed and dressed quickly, and made it down to the dining room just after 8:00. Mrs Hindle was waiting for him, but there was no sign of Mr Jones.

She offered Tom eggs, bacon, sausage, 'but I know you don't like beans' and then went into the kitchen to cook. When she returned a few minutes later, she put the plate down in front of Tom and sat in the chair opposite him.

'I just wanted to thank you again for your help yesterday morning.'

Tom felt confused. 'Mrs Hindle…?'

'Call me Denise, love, please. Mr Jones had been so pleasant when he checked in, and then he turned like that. I know I spilt all that coffee on his lap, but he was getting so aggressive. If you hadn't been here... Well, I really did think he was going to get violent. I suspect he's a drinker - or worse.'

Tom was about to say he hadn't been there yesterday morning, he hadn't arrived until the afternoon, when he realised she was right. This was his second breakfast in the guest house; he'd been there two nights. Most of the previous day was blurry and indistinct, but he did recall the incident with Mr Jones. Tom was somehow there but not there. It was if someone else had been occupying his body, controlling his thoughts and actions. He had interceded. Mr Jones had backed down and the atmosphere calmed.

'Cheeky so-and-so left without paying of course' complained Mrs Hindle.

Chapter nine

The train back to London was packed with boisterous and noisy football fans on their way down to a big match at Wembley. Tom would normally have found them intimidating but his mind was focussed elsewhere. He was going round in circles trying to reconcile the confusion in his mind. He desperately wanted to ignore it and dismiss everything as alcohol-fuelled fantasy. But it was all too intense, too real. Maybe he was going mad. At what point did dreams become psychotic hallucinations?

There was a third option that kept coming back, nagging and picking at his imagination. What if he had, somehow, been in that trench? Every time the thought came back he tried to block it out. There lay the true madness.

As the train sped past the castle he'd seen on the outbound journey, he finally reached a decision. It was one of those decisions that is thinly disguised procrastination, he recognised that, but it gave him some respite from the turmoil in his head.

In the trench, he felt he knew the names of all the men and also of their wives and children. That roll call was now lost to him - that in itself said something - but there were two names he did remember, burnt into his mind like their hideous fates: his friend Bill Lord and the boy soldier Alfie Langport. There would be records of First World War fatalities. If he could find a William Lord and Alfred Langport dying on or around the same day then… No, he said to himself, that was wrong. That was exactly what he mustn't find.

He'd left his washing on a clothes horse in the kitchen, and his flat smelt damp as he entered the front door. The usual pile of junk mail lay on the mat, but he stepped over it, propped his case against the hall radiator and walked straight into his cramped living room. He pulled open the thin curtains and a ration of extra light came in from the north facing window. As ever, everything was tidy and in place. The remote control lay beneath the TV, lying perfectly parallel to the bottom of the set. His aging laptop sat on the coffee table, squarely aligned to its corner. One thing he didn't miss about Amanda was her inability to put things away. He powered up the laptop and waited impatiently for the columns of icons to take their allotted positions on the screen.

He selected Google, ignored the animated graphic celebrating some obscure artist's centenary, and typed *first world war death records* into the box below. Adverts for family history sites topped the results, but his eye was drawn to *Commonwealth War Graves Commission* and below that, *CWGC - Find War Dead*. He found himself being offered a search across a database of 1.7 million men and women of the Commonwealth forces who died during the two world wars.

He typed *Lord, William* and selected *First World War*. Almost immediately three pages of names were returned, but scrolling through he found only two men who had served in the East Lancashire Regiment. He wrote down their dates of death and then entered a new search.

Langport, Alfred, First World War returned a solitary record. He was a private and in the East Lancashire Regiment. He died in June 1917. His age had been left blank.

The date of death didn't correlate with those of the two soldiers named William Lord, but the statistician in Tom made him focus on something else. He repeated his previous search but omitted the forename, Alfred. There was still only one match. Only one soldier named

Langport had died in the whole of the First World War and his name was Alfred. And he'd served in the right regiment.

Tom turned some thoughts over in his head. Langport was clearly an unusual surname. So what were the chances of its one fatality being called Alfred *and* serving in the East Lancs? Alfred was more common a hundred years ago, but surely no more so than Albert, George, John, William, Edward, Fred, Henry and a dozen other names. Tom googled *number of british regiments in first world war* and found a site that listed them alphabetically. He quickly totted up at least 150. On that basis, the chances of a soldier called Langport being an Alfred and serving in the East Lancs could be thousands to one. Maybe Alfred was a popular Christian name among the Langports, maybe the family was clustered in Lancashire, but the fact remained, it was all too much of a coincidence.

Dealing with factual data and figures made Tom feel rational again. It seemed clear that he could not have randomly imagined the name Alfred Langport; he must have come across it somewhere before. If he could understand how it had got into his subconscious then he would be on the way to regaining his sanity. Had Alfred Langport been mentioned on a TV programme or news article about the First World War? Perhaps he'd done something heroic? Perhaps he'd been given as an example of an underage soldier who'd seen service in the trenches? That might easily have seeded Tom's dream. And Tom was becoming sure it was a dream: it was the only sane explanation.

He googled *Alfred Langport*. Apart from establishing there was a town in Somerset called Langport, the name drew a complete blank. He tried *Alfie Langport*, *A Langport*, just *Langport*, different spellings. He read web page after web page but still found nothing. There was no mention in news stories, online encyclopaedias or history sites.

Tom leant back on his sofa. Where did this leave him? Doubt began to creep back into his mind, but he fought against it. Alfred Langport still seemed to hold the key. The Commonwealth War Graves Commission records showed that at least one Alfred Langport had existed. He died in 1917 on the Western Front but he seemed to have left no other, substantial trace - certainly on the modern world and the Internet - and Tom struggled to see where he might have come across the name. Maybe it was from something long forgotten in his childhood.

His thoughts returned to Burnley, and for some reason an image formed of himself as a young boy, no more than four years old. He was wearing a neat suit, shorts, jacket and tie, and standing on a wall next to an elderly couple. They were also smartly dressed; the lady was carrying some flowers and the gentleman had his arm around Tom to stop him falling.

The image was in black and white. Tom wasn't sure he actually remembered being at his grandparents' wedding. He'd seen that photograph a hundred times on his grandmother's mantlepiece. Perhaps it had taken the place of a genuine memory.

His father's father had been widowed and was marrying the woman who Tom would grow up knowing as Grandma. Tom vaguely recalled Grandad always seeming rather stern, but perhaps that was because his health was failing. He died just a year into the marriage. Grandma lived on for nearly twenty years, and Tom remembered her fondly as a happy, warm woman who treated him and his sister with love and kindness.

As he thought of his grandfather, he realised he had another name from his nightmare in the trenches. As well as Bill Lord and Alfie Langport there was... Thomas Haworth, Corporal Thomas Haworth of the East Lancs.

What if Tom hadn't simply cast himself as the lead character in his own drama? He vaguely recalled his Grandma telling him that Grandad had fought in the First

World War. And Tom had been named after his grandfather.

Chapter ten

Tom's sister had married a software engineer from Minnesota. They'd met while he was working in Manchester, and when his two-year assignment ended, she went back with him to the American Midwest. Rochester was a city of 100,000 inhabitants and boasted a hundred parks and its own symphony orchestra. Its economy was centred on the prestigious Mayo Clinic, and the hospital's buildings dominated the downtown blocks. Patients, including kings and several ex-Presidents, would fly in from all over the globe to land at Rochester International Airport. The waffle-iron grid of long, straight roads stretched out of town, and in the long, hot days of summer, ran through endless golden corn fields. From November to March, the mercury shrank deep into the thermometer and everything was buried under thick snow. Sarah learnt to ski, and when the thaw came, spent her weekends canoeing down the Zumbro River or in one of the state's claimed 10,000 lakes. She loved the lifestyle, the affluence of American society and she loved the people. Her husband earned good money at the plant, and as a trained nurse, she also funded their American dream working at the Mayo. She'd had a career break when Josh and Janey were young, but now they were teenagers, she was back on the wards. Despite she and Jim having put on a few pounds over the years, they were both healthy, fulfilled and happy. Any homesickness she'd suffered had faded after her parents had passed away. Jim was promising to take the kids on a European trip to find their roots in England; however, Sarah felt no strong urge to go back. She was happy for the Tower of London and

Buckingham Palace to be on the itinerary; she was less sure about the derelict mills of Burnley.

When they did visit London, she would at least be able to catch up with her big brother. He'd never been good at keeping in touch, and she felt guilty that she didn't make more of an effort herself. Despite his assurances, she knew that the breakdown of his marriage had hit him hard and she suspected there were other problems that he wasn't revealing. His new choice of career seemed particularly strange. If only Tom and Amanda had had children, maybe they'd have stayed together, or perhaps it would have given Tom more to live for. Sarah had no doubt that, by contrast, Amanda would be doing just fine on her own.

The SUV's tires scrubbed noisily on the yard as Jim left for work at 6:45 am as usual. Sarah's shift at the clinic didn't start until 10:00 am, so she lay in bed and clicked her iPad into life to check her emails. There was the usual selection of gossip and social events, but one message had arrived in the early hours and sat at the top of the page.

Hey Sis!

Hope you, Jim and the kids are well, and that you haven't been buried under snow, or overrun by wild mustangs, or infested by rattlers, or stampeded by longhorns, or swamped by alligators, or overcome by skunk, or bothered by buffalo, or gnawed by gophers, or ravaged by raccoons... Ok, that's enough feeble American wildlife based humour; I guess you're not 11 anymore. Chastised by chipmunks? No, perhaps not.

I'm fine. Sorry for not emailing sooner. I know it was my turn, but things have been pretty hectic at work. I finally took a break and guess what? I decided to give the private island in the Maldives a miss this year and went to Burnley instead. They've knocked a few more things down, but the place still feels the same. I don't know how you can keep away.

Going back there got me thinking about our family history and how little I really know. It isn't something I remember speaking about with Mum or Dad, and with them dying relatively young, the opportunity's gone.

For reasons I'd rather not bore you with, I want to look at the Haworths rather than Mum's side. No, not for some patrilineal (I looked it up) male bias, Mrs Larsson, but let's just say, because I'm interested in the First World War at the moment and I know Dad's dad fought in it. I'd like to find out more about him, and from a military point of view, what regiment he was in and where he served. Mum's dad was younger, of course, and was a policeman during WWII.

This is all I know about the Haworths:

Dad had one sister, Letty, who was several years older than him but died when she was relatively young. Dad's dad was called Thomas, and I was named after him. Grandma Anne wasn't his first wife. He was a widower and married her when I was about four. I sort of remember the wedding, but you'd have been a babe in arms. I'm not even sure what Dad's real mother was called. I was born before she died, but only just. For some reason I think she was called Anne as well, but I may be confused. On the other hand, there's no law against a man marrying two women with the same name - as long as it's not at the same time. Ha ha.

And that's it, the sum total of my knowledge of the Haworth family tree. It's pathetic really. Some people can trace their ancestry back to the Tudors.

I know you've got the old photo albums and I suspect there are some clues there? Also, you've always been brighter than me and probably picked up much more when we were kids.

There you go, a challenge for you. I expect a complete Haworth family history by return email including Grandad's full service record.

Love to Jim, Josh and Janey. And to you, Sis. x
PS Just a long shot - does the name Alfred or Alfie Langport ring any bells?

Dear Tommy

Thanks for the email. It was so good to hear from you, and for once, you wrote more than a couple of sentences.

That said, there wasn't a lot about you. 'I'm fine' doesn't tell me much. You may be my big brother, but I do worry how you are and how you're coping now that bitch wife has left you. Sorry, I know you won't hear a word against her, but I never liked the pushy cow. And not just because she was taller and skinnier than me!

I'll keep this bit brief as I know you don't like me wittering on about how wonderful things are here in the US of A. We're all fit and happy. Jim's in line for promotion and may soon be running his own department. I'm still tending to the wealthy sick and Josh and Janey are getting straight As at school. They've obviously got their father's brains - and yours - rather than mine.

So, what you really want to know is Haworth family history. This is what I remember and what I've found looking through the old photo albums:

There's that really sweet picture of you at Grandad and Grandma Anne's wedding - the one that was on her mantelpiece. I'm sure you haven't forgotten that. You're wearing the cutest of little suits. Grandad's in his mid 70s at least, but Grandma Anne looks quite a few years younger.

There are only a few photos from when Dad was growing up. He's on his own or with his sister in most of them. I definitely recognise Grandad in one, but there are several people I don't know and they're not named. It's the old story - whoever stuck the photos in knew who everyone was and never thought to label them.

There's a picture of Dad, I'm pretty sure, as a toddler with a woman who is presumably his mother. It's so dark you struggle to make out her face. I can't tell if the photo was originally underexposed or if it's blackened with time.

There's Mum and Dad's wedding album, of course. Our grandparents are all nice and clear in that. Dad definitely got his looks from his mother rather than his father, though she'd gone grey and put on a fair amount of weight by that time. I fear I may have inherited her build - I'm not sure you'll recognise me next time you see me.

Everyone always said you took after Grandad, but it's really striking when you see him as a young man before he lost his hair. It could be you, Tommy, it really could. There are a couple of pictures of him in army uniform. He looks like he's in his early twenties. The first one shows a smiling, fresh-faced soldier, all neat and pressed with a smart cap on his head. He's grown one of those dapper little moustaches. There's a photographer's stamp on the back saying it was taken in a studio in Burnley, presumably just before he went overseas. Then there's one on which he's written 'Your Tom, France' across the bottom. His uniform has got quite scruffy and he looks so tired, poor lad. The moustache has gone too.

Our scanner's on the blink or I'd have sent you copies rather than trying to describe them. Jim says he'll take them into work tomorrow and try to find time to scan them there. From what you said, it's the army photos you're most interested in?

As for what I remember myself, Mum was always talking to me about her family, but Dad never did somehow. Grandma Anne always gave the impression that Dad and Grandad were very close, but I assume she never met Grandad's first wife and certainly never mentioned her. Mum did once or twice. I know she didn't like her at all. You know Mum never swore or used bad language? She must have thought I was out of the house, but I remember hearing her tell Dad something like: "The reason you don't talk to your relations is that your mother fell out with them all. The woman was a f*****g bitch!" I was quite shocked at the time.

Funny how people called Tom Haworth tend to marry f*****g bitches, isn't it? Oops, there I go again.

That's about all I can offer you in terms of the Haworths. Jim says lots of service records are online these days. You just need to subscribe to one of those family history sites. We're still planning that big trip to Europe next year, but you know you're always welcome over here at anytime. Jim can have another go at teaching you to canoe. And Tommy, I forget sometimes, but you were the kindest big brother a girl could have. If you ever need me, just ask and I'll get on the next plane. Jim and the kids can cope without me and the wealthy sick can stuff themselves up their gold-plated catheters.

There you go, sentiment over. Love to England and love to you.
Sarah xxx
PS Chastised by chipmunks?!
PPS Almost forgot. Never heard of Alfie Langport.

Chapter eleven

Sarah's email arrived late in the afternoon. There had been no food in the flat and Tom was just back from a shopping trip. Without a car he had to use the small supermarket on the high street; he didn't need much these days and could easily carry home a week's worth of supplies.

Today's load had been a little heavier and somewhat more expensive. The culprit sat in front of him on the coffee table, unopened.

He'd put the tins and packages neatly away before checking his laptop. His spirits were raised when he saw there was a new message in his inbox, but its contents gave him little information that he didn't already know. Perhaps he would be able identify a regimental badge or get some other clue when the scanned photos arrived.

His sister's offer to fly over made him emotional. He wasn't sure she truly meant it, and she knew he would never ask, but it made him realise how much he missed her and how alone he was.

He recognised that he'd never worked hard enough at making and keeping friends. He used to go for a drink with his colleagues at the bank but he'd lost touch after his forced resignation. He didn't really get on with anyone at his new job, and it was difficult to socialise when you were supposed to be avoiding pubs and bars. The circle of acquaintances he'd inhabited with Amanda was always made up of ambitious high-flyers in her mould, not his. There was Dave, of course. Tom had known him since university, but Dave was a hardcore drinker and Tom hadn't been in touch with him for months. Tom realised he had no-one to confide in, and even if he did, would he really want to share the crazy ideas disturbing the balance of his mind? He pictured Amanda's face if he told her. It brought a wry smile to his lips.

He was alone with his only friend, who doubled as his worst enemy. The bottle of cheap, own-brand scotch silently called to him with a siren's song of escape, calm and sleep. He told himself he would be sober tomorrow. He broke open the seal, settled back on the sofa and said goodbye to the rest of the day.

Chapter twelve

There was a sudden jolt and Tom found himself on a firm upholstered seat with his head leaning against a cold window. The only light came from outside. It took a second for his eyes to adjust, and a gloomy station scene came into focus. It was nighttime and the few lamps seemed to flicker and glow. There was a hissing sound coming from somewhere, and the air smelt of damp smoke.

'Come on soldier. This is your stop. It's Preston. I'm sure we'll be here a while, like every other bloody station we've been through, but you don't want to hang about.'

Tom thanked the middle-aged man sat to his left and pulled his pack down from the luggage rack above their heads. He slid down the carriage window, leaned out to turn the door handle and then stepped down onto the platform.

He recognised the station, the footbridge and the ornate ironwork, but even in the dim light he could tell it was black and grimy. But why shouldn't it be? Steam locomotives spewed out smoke and soot; why would it be anything else?

Once again, Tom became aware of two voices in his head. One was the battle weary soldier who'd just spent hours stopping and starting on a painfully slow train running to wartime schedules. The other was an indistinct, ghost consciousness that saw sleek electric trains and a station canopy supported by columns and trusses in clean white, green and red. Once again, Tom pushed the irrational thoughts away.

Throwing his pack over his shoulder, he hurried over the footbridge and across to the platforms of the

Lancashire and Yorkshire Railway. They were deserted apart from a young woman, about his own age, wearing a dark uniform far smarter than his own.

'What time's the Burnley train, miss?'

The porter tilted her head apologetically. 'I'm sorry, soldier. You've missed it. There won't be one until eight o'clock tomorrow now.'

'Surely they run later than this?'

'The timetables are all over the place. You know how it is. Half the drivers and firemen are off fighting; half the trains are requisitioned for war work. I am sorry. You won't be able to get anywhere until the morning. I've got a nice fire going in the waiting room; you can settle yourself down in there. I'll make sure you've plenty of coal.'

Tom's head dropped. The funeral was at 10:00 am. He'd been given leave to travel home from France and the chances of getting there in time now seemed remote. Even when he reached Burnley he still had to make his way up into the hills. Perhaps he should have gone via Manchester after all? He briefly considered tightening up his laces and marching all the way but he knew it was 25, maybe 30 miles. There was hardly any moon to see by and his old thigh wound had been troubling him recently. His leg wouldn't cope with a walk that far.

He thanked the porter and followed her into the waiting room. She stoked the fire and then bade him goodnight. He wrapped himself tightly in his greatcoat and tried to get comfortable on the hard bench. If he managed any sleep he was unaware of it and spent the night staring into the dancing flames. His thoughts were dark and confused.

They were coming down from the upper graveyard when Tom arrived. He was sticky with sweat and noticeably limping from the pain in his right leg. At first he thought the whole village was there but soon noticed the scarcity of the younger men. As he walked through the crowd, he received sympathetic smiles, brief greetings and expressions of condolence, and then found himself standing in front of Ann Lord. Her face was as beautiful as ever, but her dark chocolate eyes looked up at him full of ice.

'Ann, how are you? How's Bill?'

'My husband is still in hospital. He's still suffering a lot of pain. I see him when I can. They let me wheel him around the gardens in one of them bath chairs. He's a medical miracle, apparently. They never thought he'd last this long. They're very proud of him, and in return, he hates them. He hates everything really.'

'Oh, Ann, I'm so sorry, lass.'

'Yes, Tom, I'm sure you are. Poor Bill! That's what everyone says. What about me? What about poor Ann? I'm a young woman, Tom. And a better looking one than all these others with their perfect husbands and beaus. I don't deserve this, this so-called life. The sooner he...' She stopped herself and glared at Tom resentfully before starting to walk away. 'If you'll forgive me, I've got to get back to the mill. The yarn won't spin itself.'

Tom watched her leave and then looked up to see the final group of people descending the steep tree-lined path. The minister led the way, closely followed by Clara. Her eyes were full of tears, but her face broke into a broad smile when she saw the tall soldier amongst the mourners.

The distant, vague shadow Tom of an unimaginable future came to the fore. Though his other self had known her all his life, it was as if he was looking at her for the first time. In her features he saw a blueprint of every girl he'd ever been attracted to. From a short distance she could be mistaken for his wife. But there was a gentleness and a kindness in that face that Amanda never had.

Clara rushed up to him and took his hands in hers. He felt a surge of happiness that seemed to block his ability to speak. The future Tom faded into the background and his mind returned to the present.

'Oh, Tom! I didn't think you were coming. It's so wonderful to see you.' She glanced over her shoulder before whispering, 'We'll get together later; you need to see your dad first. He won't show it, but he's so upset. I don't know how he'll cope without your mother. Try to talk to him for once, Tom. Please.'

Her mid-brown eyes held Tom's for a second longer and then she released his hands and left.

The minister was saying his final words to Tom's father. 'We'll all be praying for you, George.' He smiled and stood back as Tom came over.

'I'm sorry I'm late, Dad. There were no trains last night.'

'Never mind, Son. You're here. That's what matters. It would have meant a lot to your mum.'

Tom heard an emptiness in his father's voice where he'd sensed only coldness before. 'Dad, how are you? It must have come as a terrible shock.'

'I'm fine, Son. She's in a better place. It was a release when it came. She'd been ill for a while. Suffered towards the end.' His voice faltered briefly. 'She wouldn't tell you in her letters. She said you'd got enough to worry about. Look, you'll want to go up and see the grave? She's in with little Sarah Alice.'

Tom looked at the grey-black stone path that led up the slope and experienced a strange but acute reluctance. 'I've seen enough graves, Dad. Maybe later. I just need to be with you and my sisters. That's what Mum would have wanted.'

By the early afternoon, Tom and his father were alone in the front parlour. The room was kept for best, perhaps a visit from the minister or the in-laws, and Tom was sat for almost the first time in the sturdy wooden armchair closest to the fire. Sensing that father and son should be left to talk, Ethelina had taken her two younger sisters out onto the hills in the hope that open skies and fresh air would raise their spirits.

Back in the house, both men were deep in thought staring at the floor. Tom's father broke the silence. 'Your mother was a good woman, Tom. A strong woman. She carried me, you know. It's going to be hard.'

Though he'd known it since the grim letter had arrived in France, Tom was suddenly hit by the realisation he would never again see the woman who had been so important to him for so long. He felt an almost overwhelming urge to cry. He managed to hold it back but not before taking a sharp, audible gasp of air.

'I'm sorry, Dad. What must you think of me? I almost broke down like a baby.'

'Nay, lad. It's right. She was your mother. You and her were so close. No need to apologise to me.' After a short pause his father continued. 'She was so very proud of you, you know that. And I am too, Tom. I've never told you. I guess I hoped you knew. I couldn't cope with losing you as well. This damned war...' For the first time in over 40 years, a tear made its way down the older man's face.

Tom leant over and put a hand on his father's knee. 'They won't get me, Dad. I'm a canny old soldier now. I'm one of the beggers who keeps his head down, volunteers for nothing. This war can't go on forever. I'll be back in that weaving shed before you know it.'

When the three sisters returned, George Haworth insisted his son call on Clara. Not long after, and for the second time in a day, Tom found himself sitting in a smart front parlour. Mrs Hargreaves had made them a cup of tea and left the young couple to talk.

'How's your dad, Tom?'

'Like you said, he's really upset.'

'And you, how do you feel? It must be awful to lose your mum.'

'It is, but I'm not a child anymore, Clara. Everyone loses their parents at some time. It's the way of the world.' He paused whilst he considered the accuracy of what he had just said. 'Well, it doesn't always work like that, I suppose. Wars in particular change the rules. Clara, there's something I've been thinking about, something I need to tell you.' He took a sip of tea to give him time to assemble the right words. 'I'm not like you. I've never really thought about other people's feelings. I've never been a kind man. It's always been about what I wanted, what I had to achieve.'

'You're strong, Tom. A woman looks for strength in a man. And what about that time Frank Hindle was being set upon by Jim Bradshaw? Everyone else was scared of getting involved. You were the only one who stepped in. You know I've always admired you for that. That showed you cared.'

He shook his head. 'I've never admitted this to you before, but I didn't do that for Frank. I was trying to prove something to myself. What a big man I was. You... you wouldn't understand. But now I do want to show that I can care. I want to do something kind. Just for once.'

Clara looked at him quizzically, uncertain where the conversation was going.

He took her hands and looked into her eyes. 'Clara, this war... It's never going to stop. It's been years and we're still stuck in the same stretch of mud and filth and devastation. There are these enormous battles, we suffer thousands of casualties, and if we're lucky, move forward a few hundred yards. In a matter of days or weeks the Germans just take it back again. They call it a war of attrition; we're just wearing each other down. It will only end when everyone's dead. When the shells and the bullets run out they'll have us fighting with bayonets and clubs and our bare hands.'

Clara interjected. 'What about the Americans? The Manchester Guardian says they've only sent a few men so far, but it's a country of limitless resources. They've introduced conscription so it's only a matter of time before they start to make a real difference. It will end, Tom. You have to have faith.'

'Faith is one thing I've lost, lass. The only thing I believe in now is that I've got hardly any chance of coming home alive. And if I do, I'll be like Bill, a pitiful wreck, no man at all.'

Clara hadn't seen Bill since his return from France, but what she'd heard of his injuries made her squeeze her eyes closed in horror.

'I'm sorry, Clara, I don't want to upset you. That's the last thing I want. As I said, I want to do at least one kind thing in my life. I want to release you from your promise. I don't want you waiting for a man who isn't likely to come home, and most of all, I don't want you tied to some hopeless cripple like Ann Lord is. You should have seen the hatred in her eyes when she saw me at the funeral.'

'Why would she hate you? You didn't cause Bill's wounds.'

'I was there when it happened. He begged me to shoot him and I hadn't the guts.'

'Tom, it would have been wicked to do that! Absolutely wicked!'

'Oh, Clara! I am wicked, can't you see? The things I've done in France. The blood I've got on my hands. You can't imagine the brutality of a what a soldier is expected to do at the front.' He felt a sneer distort his features. 'When you kill an enemy you're told it's war, it's heroic, it's just. God's on our side, after all. But if I end my best friend's suffering, it's some kind of immoral crime.'

Clara said nothing and Tom felt her grip on his hands loosen as he carried on with his half-rehearsed speech.

'I want to release you from your promise. I want you to find someone else. I love you Clara, please believe that, but you deserve a happiness that I can never see myself giving you.' He took another sip from his tea. Clara maintained her silence and the look on her face was indecipherable. 'I know there aren't many men around who aren't at the front or already spoken for. I suppose there's Frank Hindle; it wasn't the biggest surprise he failed the army medical. No, you can do better than him. Mr Chambers, though, he's a fine man. A minister needs a wife. We both know he's always admired you and I thought—'

'Enough.' Clara spoke softly but there was an incontestable authority in her voice. 'You're upset. Your mother has just died. You're tired, my love. I wish I could save you from this awful war and bring you home, but I can't. All I can do is pray for you and your safe return. To me. I'll be here for you whatever. And when you do come home, we'll never be parted again. Now, I don't want to hear this talk again. Ever.'

The emotion he'd managed to hold back in front of his father finally overcame him. Tom sank to his knees and buried his head in Clara's lap.

Later they walked up to the reservoir together, just as they had that last few days before war was declared. Tom found it difficult to talk: his mind was dominated by terrible images that he did not want to share. Clara instinctively understood and they were content just to be in each other's company. When they came back past the church, she suggested they visit his mother's grave; he again felt that peculiar sense of unease and declined.

It was dark when he said goodnight and returned home. His father was waiting for him, sitting alone in the front parlour. The girls had gone to bed early after their long, painful day.

Tom sat down and his father smiled in greeting. Leaning over, he opened the wooden sideboard door and pulled out a dusty bottle. Two glasses were already waiting on the table.

After drinking a toast 'To mother', the two men sat in wordless communion. They listened to the ticking of the mantel clock and stared at the level of the warming amber liquid as it sank gradually downwards in the bottle.

Chapter thirteen

Tom felt for the switch as the alarm screeched discordantly. His wife had preferred to be woken by a mellow, middle-of-the-road radio station, but he needed something more insistent. His heart began to race and then slowed as he stared at the ten red LED bars that formed the numbers 7 and 15. Their glow lit the room and reassured him of where he was. When he was. Initially, he felt only relief from knowing he did not have a train to catch. A train that would take him back to the nightmare of the trenches. Soon, though, his mood was tempered by a sense of loss. He had met, literally it seemed, the woman of his dreams, and she was gone, lost in time and in the folds of his fragile mind.

When Tom arrived at work, the girls in the office greeted him awkwardly. Then Carl Singleton walked in, and they all became transfixed to their computer screens as if an urgent email had just been copied to each of them. Carl saw who else was in the room and appeared unnerved. His look of discomfort was exaggerated by his upper lip, which was bruised and swollen. He quickly picked up the papers from his pigeonhole and left.

'A word please, Tom.'

Jimmy Mills was standing at the door of his office. 'Do you mind coming in for a chat? Please take a seat.' Jimmy closed the door behind him and sat facing Tom across a large polished mahogany desk. 'I'm sure you know what this is about, Tom.'

A short series of images, like the scenes from a comic book story, flashed into Tom's mind. Instead of speech bubbles, disjointed snippets of conversation provided the narrative links.

He was alone in one of the classrooms setting up the projector. The fluorescent lights were on, presumably because it was gloomy outside. He could sense he was hungover but sober. The door was opening.

'Morning, wanker.'

Carl's voice was full of arrogance and condescension. Tom felt himself bristle in anger and he heard words spit from his own mouth.

'Who the beggery do you think you're talking to?'

The response changed Carl's sneering expression to one of confusion. It was the look of someone trying to gauge how far a normally timid man might go after making such an uncharacteristically aggressive challenge. Perhaps there was also recognition that the other man was somewhat larger than himself. Any analysis was fleeting; Tom saw the expression become shock when Carl found himself thrown against the wall. He lunged back, but Tom's arm and fist arced round to catch Carl full in the face. The final image was of Carl sitting back against the wall, bloodied, frightened and with a palm raised in a gesture of surrender.

The drama played out in Tom's head in a fraction of a second, and then his attention returned to his boss and the response he was waiting for.

'It's about yesterday, Jimmy. The incident with Carl.'

'Correct. And to state the obvious, it is totally unacceptable for one of my members of staff to assault another.'

'I agree. I don't know what to say. I can't believe I acted like that. It's as if it was someone else in that classroom.' Tom took a deep breath and gathered his thoughts. 'If I'm honest, Jimmy, I've been bullied, on and off, all my life. It's made me hate bullies, and now I seem to have become one, some kind of bloody thug.'

'I wouldn't go that far, Tom. I understand there was a fair amount of provocation. Carl can be an unpleasant so-and-so at times. He would never have got away with talking to me the way he did to you.'

'Yes, but when you look past all that swagger, you can see he's just a short, fat man with a chip on his shoulder. Over the course of his life, he's probably been picked on more than me.'

Jimmy hesitated while he considered his options. He reached a conclusion and began explaining it slowly and carefully. 'Okay. To a large extent I blame myself. I should have done something earlier when I heard on the office grapevine that he'd been bragging about how he'd put you in your place. I was tied up trying to negotiate that new contract and I guess I thought it would blow over. The problem I've got is, if he makes a formal complaint, I will have no alternative but to sack you.'

Tom nodded. He was in immediate danger of losing his livelihood but was uncharacteristically calm. He had accepted responsibility for his actions and would face the consequences. For once in his life he felt no fear or apprehension, perhaps because he had seen much darker prospects in his dreams.

A satisfied smile began to emerge on Jimmy's face as he expanded on his decision. 'I'm going to have a chat with Carl. I'll explain your remorse - which I can see is genuine - and say I'd prefer not to take it any further. There was no-one else present, so I'm going to suggest we treat it as a private argument between two grown men who are big enough and ugly enough to take it on the chin. No pun intended. I can be a very persuasive man, particularly if I hint that Carl's own job might be on the line for starting the trouble in the first place. Leave it with me. But, Tom, it ends here. Understand? I'll take a very different view if it happens again.'

Tom's Saturday mornings followed one of two patterns. If he was drinking, they would be spent in bed, nursing a hangover and feeling sick and guilty. If he was off the booze, he would allow himself a short lie-in before heading off to his local high street. When he woke this Saturday, the sun was shining through the curtains and he felt the wary optimism of a man who was starting to take control of his life. He hadn't had a drink yesterday, or the day before, or the day before that. He wouldn't have one today.

He usually did the bulk of his shopping, such as it was, on Thursday evenings. On Saturdays he would just buy some fresh bread and a paper. (His family had always read the Guardian. Whilst Tom didn't always agree with its politics, he liked the crossword; it was difficult enough to provide a diversion but not so cryptic that he would waste hours obsessively trying to interpret the last few clues.) Before the bakery and the newsagent, however, his routine would take him into his local library.

It was a fine Georgian building whose blue plaque declared that it was once the home of an operatic tenor who had been a favourite of Handel. Purchased by the local council around the turn of the last century, its extensive gardens had been lost beneath two streets of terraced social housing. It was set some distance away from the main shops, in an area that had been more prominent when the old water works was the main local employer. Now many people lived in the district for years without being aware of the library's existence, despite it being one of the largest in the borough.

The original house dated from the 1770s, but it had been extended during the reign of Victoria and again in the 1980s. That last development had been done by a talented young architect who had sympathetically linked the various ground floor rooms using broad open archways. The building faced south, and large French windows and a partial glass roof flooded its spacious interior with light and warmth. It was one of Tom's favourite places and a refuge from the pressures he often felt in his everyday life.

This Saturday he had come in for a specific reason, not just to browse the shelves. Like every modern library, some of the floor space had been given over to computer terminals. These were free for members to use, and one of the roles of library staff was to provide basic IT education for anyone who needed it. On a previous visit, Tom had seen an advertisement for training in family history research. It had never interested him in the past, but recent events meant it was something he now felt compelled to explore.

As was often the case, the library was quiet with only a handful of people amongst the neat rows of wooden shelving. Tom looked around and then approached the man he had always assumed was the senior librarian, mainly on account of his age. Tom thought he must be several years older than himself, though when you looked closely at his face it wasn't quite as worn as his grey hair and beard suggested. The man was on his knees in the non-fiction section carefully slotting a large and heavy art book into its correct Dewey Decimal position on a low shelf.

Tom coughed. 'Hi. Sorry to interrupt. Are you still doing the family history sessions? I came in hoping to do some research myself and don't really know where to start.'

The man looked up. 'Yes, we're still doing them. Erm, you normally have to book a session in advance, but I've had a cancellation this morning and we're really quiet, so I can probably fit you in now. Give me a second and I'll check with the manager.'

The man pushed the book into place, stood up and walked over to an attractive young woman half his age sitting at the enquiry desk. After a brief conversation he returned smiling. 'Yes, that should be fine. I normally allow an hour, but with our tea breaks coming up, we'll have to limit it to 30 minutes. Hopefully that will give us enough time. I assume you've used a PC before?'

'Yes, every day. At home, at work. I'm pretty computer literate.'

'In which case, we should be okay.'

Tom was shown over to a desk in the far corner of the library. It had a single computer, but space for two chairs. Tom sat directly in front of the keyboard, the librarian off to one side. After asking Tom to log on using his personal library card number, his instructor started with a list of questions that he'd clearly asked many time before.

'Have you done any family history research previously and, or, how far back can you trace your ancestors at the moment? It gives us a head start if you have some names and dates that take us to 1911 or before. That's the most recent census available. Oh, and where were your ancestors born?'

'The people I'm interested in are from Lancashire, an area called the Forest of Rossendale. Though I don't know why it's called that. There are hardly any trees, certainly not up on the moors' replied Tom.

The librarian smiled knowingly. 'Forest was a term introduced by the Normans for a royal hunting ground. It didn't necessarily imply woodland. That's something the word has come to mean over time.'

Tom nodded. 'That's really interesting, thank you, I've often wondered. Going back to your questions, I haven't done any family history research before, but I'm really interested in finding out about my grandfather, Tom Haworth, and his family. He was in the Great War, so would definitely have been around in 1911.'

'Okay, good, that gives us something to work with. Let's make a start'.

The librarian carried on speaking in the steady flow of someone well rehearsed. 'Family history is big business on the Internet. Several rival companies have been digitising genealogical data sources and have built websites around them. Unlike most of the Web, you have to pay to access these sites. It's fair enough, the companies have had to invest a considerable amount of effort and resources, and family history research has been transformed from what it was ten or twenty years ago. Progress was very slow back in the days of paper records and microfilm. All the same, it still requires time and patience to build a family tree. All I can hope to achieve today is to get you started.'

Tom nodded again and listened attentively.

'Okay. There's a special library edition of one of the leading family history sites. We subscribe to it, so provided you are on one of our computers, here in the library, you can use it here for free.'

The librarian showed Tom the link for accessing the site and then continued. 'There's a wide set of different databases, spanning birth, marriage and death indexes; censuses; parish registers; military records; immigration; phone books; and so on. They're from all over the world and being added to all the time. There's so much information it can seem a bit overwhelming at first. To my mind, there are two methods of hunting down what you want…'

The librarian hesitated. 'Okay. We don't have much time and I'm talking too much. Let's get stuck in and try an example of the first method. We'll simply type a name into the home page, search across all those collections of data, and see what comes up. Couldn't be easier. Do you want to key the name in?'

Tom began entering *Haworth* into the surname field and then stopped. 'No. Let's use someone else' he said and typed *Langport, Alfred* into the page.

After a short delay, a list of 19 records appeared on the screen.

The librarian looked surprised and then observed, 'That's not many given that we're searching all the worldwide records at this stage. Normally you have to refine the search because you've got too many matches. It must be quite an unusual name.'

Several of the results were easily dismissed as being too recent or from the wrong part of the world. They were left with four. The library's network connection was slow and it took some time to open each document. In part, they confirmed what Tom had discovered on the Commonwealth War Graves website: a Private Alfred Langport of the East Lancs regiment had died in 1917 and was subsequently awarded the standard campaign medals for everyone who saw service overseas. His birth was registered in Blackburn in the last quarter of 1901. The librarian thought the date was too late, but Tom explained that the boy had lied about his age in order to join up. The 1911 census was just a little more informative. Nine year-old Alfred was still at school. Like her only child, Mrs Victoria Langport had been born in Blackburn, but her husband, Henry, was a weaver who hailed from Somerset.

Tom felt saddened that Alfred's existence on earth, short as it was, could leave such a sparse trail. His own brief, totally unreliable recollection of a brave, but frightened boy with acne was potentially the most elucidating memorial of a long-lost life. He felt his shoulders drop. 'I'd hoped there'd be more, particularly in terms of his military service.'

'A German bombing raid struck the War Office repository in 1940. More than half the records from World War One were destroyed. Other than the medal records, I've never been able to find anything for my own relatives who saw service' explained the librarian before looking at his watch and saying with some urgency, 'Okay, time's tight, so I really must show you the other way of searching all these different collections of data. It's the way you tend to work when you've a bit more experience. Basically, you go direct to the database you're interested in rather than the scattergun approach of searching everything. How about we look for your grandfather in the 1911 census specifically?'

Tom was guided through a sequence of steps and a list of Thomas Haworths from 1911 appeared on the screen. There were two likely candidates, and the first they checked revealed a set of names that Tom recognised. He had found his grandfather.

He was looking at census form completed on the night of Sunday, April 2, 1911. The handwriting was somehow familiar. The head of the household was George Haworth, a cotton overlooker in a throstle room. He had been married to his wife, Letitia, for 19 years. She'd had five children of whom four were still living. Ethelina was the eldest, working as a spinner, then came Thomas, a 15 year-old weaver, and two younger daughters, also weavers. All were born locally. The family lived at number 8, North Street.

At this point, Tom noticed that the library manager was looking across from the other side of the room and pointing at her upheld watch. The librarian started to stand up and apologised. 'I'm sorry, I will have to leave you now. I've shown you the basics and you seem to have picked it up very quickly. I'm sure you'll be fine working your way around the website on your own. Feel free to book another session sometime if you need any more help.'

Tom expressed his gratitude and then turned back to the screen and considered the options it offered him. At the bottom was a page number and arrows facing to the left and right. He clicked on the right arrow and the occupants of number 10, North Street emerged.

Tom realised he could work his way around his grandfather's entire village by paging through the census returns household by household. A few doors from the Haworths he found the Lord family and a young weaver called William, the same age as Tom Haworth at number 8. Across the street was Percy Franklin Chambers, a

Baptist minister from Warwick, who lived alone with his housekeeper in a dwelling with a grand name rather than a number.

Tom continued on his journey as if walking down every road and knocking on every door that dark Sunday evening. In his mind he could see each house, its position against its neighbours, the way it faced the street. He was heading in a conscious, deliberate direction. At the end of one of the longer terraces he found her, Clara Hargreaves, weaver.

He sat back in his chair and stared at the image on the screen in front of him, a printed form filled in by hand over a hundred years ago. Was that her handwriting? No, too masculine, presumably her father's, but he would have shown her the document, surely? Censuses only happen every ten years. A bright young girl would be interested. Her mid-brown eyes would have read the same brief words that lay before Tom now.

It was just a piece of paper but it provided a bridge across the decades and across the generations. Clara was real and his dreams, his journeys back in time, had to be real. All the names, coincidence on coincidence, the odds were just too high for everything to be the random creation of his subconscious.

Tom sat motionless until the computer shut itself down, convinced by the lack of activity that he had got up and walked away. He continued to stare at the screen as it dimmed to black.

He had known her for a few hours. He had known her all his life. He wanted to see her again. But what was he prepared to risk?

Chapter fourteen

Once again, Tom sat in his tidy living room. The laptop had been on his knee and he placed it back on the coffee table, ensuring it sat square in the corner with its power cable tucked neatly out of sight. The photos of his grandfather had finally arrived from his sister. She was right, there was a striking resemblance, though the khaki-clad soldier looked fuller in the face and stronger. He was considerably younger after all. The regimental cap badge was slightly indistinct, but its overall shape did match that of the East Lancs. It was another piece of evidence, though nothing conclusive. It didn't really matter: Tom was already convinced. Any doubts or thoughts of madness were suppressed under the consuming, circular indecision of what was causing the phenomenon, and more pressingly, what he should do next.

Alcohol seemed like it could be the common link. Perhaps it was interacting with the medication he was still on. But how could that explain what he was experiencing? For some reason he was going back in time, having vivid dreams that were not dreams, full of people and places he didn't know but were real characters and scenes from his grandfather's life.

Maybe the answer to his dilemma lay in another bottle of whisky. He wanted to see Clara again. He wanted to drink again; God knows, he always wanted to drink, but did he dare?

Tom's rationality was warning him of the dangers, the least of which was perpetuating his addiction. No, what frightened him was not knowing where he might emerge. Would he find himself back in the mud and gore of the Western Front or was there another heartbreaking funeral or death to endure? It had not escaped him that he'd been journeying into what were surely the blackest days of the other Tom Haworth's existence. And there was something else, some intangible sense of foreboding, that scared him off.

He sat for hours thinking the same thoughts, arguing back and forth in his head, reaching the same conclusions and then dismissing them all over again. It wore him down and eventually he forced himself into his bed. He was sober. Sleepless nights through racing, repetitive thinking are no stranger to the depressive and Tom sought distraction through happier, simpler ideas. He made himself remember Amanda when they'd first met, how attractive she seemed, how he admired her confidence. He fantasised that she had come back and lay next to him now. All he had to do was reach over and he'd feel her warm body. In the morning he would explain his confusion, perhaps even come clean about his feelings for Clara. Amanda would have the answer. She always saw things in black and white, always knew what to do.

Eventually, his mind surrendered and he slept.

Chapter fifteen

He was half-lying, half-sitting. His bare feet were resting on something soft and yielding, and when he arched his toes he found that they dug into fine sand. He was in direct warm sunlight but felt a tightly buttoned suit waistcoat about his chest. He smelt the sea and could hear the faint lapping of waves interrupted by children's laughter and the echoing screech of a seagull.

His body felt stiff as he leant forward, sliding awkwardly in the slung canvas of a deck chair. He pushed the snap-brim trilby back from over his eyes. To his right, the golden beach stretched away as far as the eye could see, merging with distant pale-mauve mountains on a hazy horizon. To his left, a complicated lattice of rust-brown iron columns, girders and braces carried a high wooden deck over the sand and out to sea. Delicate pagoda-roofed kiosks were spaced along its length, and what looked like the superstructure of a fine ship sat towards the end, before a low, slender jetty stretched on to navigable depths.

On this side of the pier, he knew the crowds were always thinner and only a few clusters of people could be seen dotted across the flat open space. Those nearest the water were beginning to gather their belongings as the ripple-like waves slipped relentlessly forward and back, each time encroaching on another few inches of dry beach. The air was windless and the Irish Sea as flat as ironed cotton, its lustrous surface reflecting the blue sky and disguising the murky, grey-brown truth of gently churning sand.

With her hem hoisted to just above her knees and the saltwater stroking her ankles, Clara stood a few feet in front of him. She wore a royal-blue dress, a pale-blue cloche hat and a smile as warm as the sunshine.

'I didn't know if you were going to wake up. I thought you might drift out to sea on your deck chair' she giggled.

Tom returned a look of mock rebuke. 'As you know, I can't swim. You'd have had to come in to rescue me and that pretty dress of yours would have been ruined' he replied, his face breaking into a grin. 'I'm going to join you for a quick paddle and then we probably ought to take the chairs back. There'll be no beach left in half an hour.'

They walked back under the pier - he carrying the deck chairs, she their shoes and socks - and climbed the steep steps set into the vertical, 30-foot-tall, black basalt seawall whose top curved outwards to turn back the rollers at high tide. The promenade was crowded with refugees from the retreating shore. Tom and Clara found a space to sit and wiped the damp, clinging sand from between their toes as best they could. After donning their footwear, they joined the queue returning chairs to the uniformed attendant and then stood against the cast iron railings and looked out to sea. Tom took out a packet of cigarettes, but after a moment of indecision, slipped them back into his jacket pocket.

He felt a gentle wave of contentment wash over him. In one part of his mind he was dimly aware of a dilemma resolved, but most of all he was just happy to be on holiday, on a glorious July day in Blackpool, with Clara. It was Burnley Wakes. The town's mills had shut down en masse, and almost the entire population had decamped to Blackpool, or Morecambe, or for the most well-to-do, Southport. Those left behind saw skies clear of haze as, once a year, the chimneys lay dormant long enough for the winds to blow away the smoky clouds that hung between the hills. When the workers of Burnley went home on the Saturday of 'changeover day', they would be replaced by those of Darwen and then Blackburn. Each industrial town would take a turn, and the landladies of Blackpool would monitor the sequence through differing accents and terms of endearment. One week they would be everyone's *love*, then *petal*, then *flower*, then *ducks*, then *hen*.

Tom's youthful desire to move to the mill town of Burnley had been fulfilled, not through the fire of ambition - his time in France had doused such flames - but because of necessity. The Great War had curtailed the export of cotton to foreign markets, and other countries, particularly India and Japan, had built their own factories. They began to produce yarn and cloth more cheaply than their British equivalents and the slow decline of the Lancashire industry began. Despite the war's scything of the male workforce, the closure of one of the village mills meant Tom could only find work as a tackler by coming down from the hills.

He worked hard, earned good money and was respected by the weavers whose looms he supervised. Like most of his contemporaries, he assumed any setbacks were temporary and the boom years of King Cotton would return.

He and Clara lived in a two-up two-down terraced house whose design was replicated across a hundred other Burnley streets. It was small and basic but well-built and a cut above the dreaded back-to-backs in the poorer quarters.

Clara would have preferred the more genteel pleasures of Morecambe, but Tom loved to holiday in Blackpool. He revelled in the crowds around the Golden Mile and Central Pier, the 500 foot Tower, the trams along the seafront, and the Pleasure Beach with its American-style amusement park rides. Most of all, he enjoyed the countless pubs and bars and Clara would spend the evenings in the company of the other wives while the menfolk drank the night away.

As Clara scanned the horizon, searching in vain for the Isle of Man across the placid swell of waves, Tom turned to gaze at his wife. Despite her hat, her attractively beaked nose was starting to redden in the sun. That strange inner voice that had visited him in the past returned. It told him that he took her for granted and that happiness could be snatched away at any time. His lips moved as if someone else was forming the words.

'I'm very lucky to have you, Clara Haworth, and I love you very much.'

She looked back into his eyes with a puzzled expression. 'Tom, that's not like you. You're not the type to get affectionate.'

'I know. And if I said that kind of thing all the time you'd think I was smarmy, but just for once, I wanted you to know how I feel.'

'Well, thank you. I love you too. You know that.'

Tom smiled and nodded, then, slightly embarrassed, adjusted his trilby and changed the subject. 'So, what shall we do next? There's that new ride at the Pleasure Beach. They call it the Big Dipper. They say it makes the Velvet Coaster look like something for kiddies. We could get on a tram or we could stroll along the prom if you prefer. Maybe get some chips on the way?'

Clara looked uncomfortable. 'Do you mind if we give the Big Dipper a miss? It sounds a bit fast and frightening to me. I don't have the strongest heart in the world, you know.'

'It's not like you to be afraid of a bit of excitement, lass. You're normally game for anything. Are you alright?'

'Well, to be honest, there is something else. I wasn't going to tell you until I was sure, until I'd seen a doctor, but I've been talking to the other wives, and well, I'm normally so regular...' She looked down at her feet self-consciously before continuing. 'Well, a woman can tell.'

It was Tom's turn to look concerned. 'Tell what?'

'I think I'm going to have a baby.'

A huge smile broke on Tom's face; he put his large hands on his wife's shoulders and lowered his head so he could look into her eyes from the same level. 'That's grand news, lass. And me wanting to take you on the big, daft Dipper.'

'Oh, I'm sure I'd be fine. It's very early days, but we've been wanting a baby for so long I don't want to take any risks.'

'Nor shall we. So what would you like to do? We can just sit on the pier and listen to the band if you'd like. Or go round the menagerie in the Tower? You name it, Mrs Haworth.'

'Oh, not the menagerie. I hate to see that poor, sad lion pacing back and forwards in his little cage. Look, I know you think it's a bit dull, but I fancy a ride on the Big Wheel. It's gentle and sedate and I used to love it as a child.'

Despite his offer, part of Tom thought of objecting - he found the Big Wheel tiresome - but he was not a man to go against his word, and another side of him simply wanted to make Clara happy. 'The Big Wheel it is, Mrs Haworth.'

There was no queue as they paid their sixpences and climbed aboard an enclosed gondola the size of a railway carriage. It was one of thirty suspended from the 250 foot high Ferris wheel that stood inland from the Tower. Its slow rotation was interrupted every time a cabin reached the bottom and exchanged its passengers. For those seeking thrills, Blackpool had much more to offer and for those who wanted a view, the Tower was twice the height.

Clara sat happily by the window and stared over the rooftops. A crimson locomotive was blowing clouds of steam as it pulled a heavy train out from one of the 14 platforms of the Central Railway Station which lay almost directly below. The gondola rocked gently on its pivot every time the wheel stopped and restarted. Tom looked around the carriage and noticed chipped paint and empty seats. He doubted the wheel was making money and wondered how much longer it would survive in a town whose motto was 'Progress'.

After a stroll around the Winter Gardens, they made their way back along the side of the station to their boarding house, the grandly named Bayswater House Hotel. They took a brief rest in their room and then went down for their evening meal, sitting with friends who all lived within a few streets back home in Burnley. Despite Clara's reservations, the proud father-to-be could not resist breaking the news to the other men.

'You'll be wanting to wet the baby's head, Tom' said Bob Cropper somewhat prematurely. Bob was one of the other tacklers at Tom's mill. He was large, grey-haired man with the blotchy complexion suggestive of a heavy drinker.

'I never say no to a drink. Or two.' laughed Tom.

'The Foxhall Arms it is then?' enthused Bob.

Tom looked over at Clara. He realised that, for once in his life, he was seeking her approval. Her doleful expression suggested it would not be given willingly.

After they'd eaten, he took her to one side in the lounge. 'You don't mind if I have a couple with the lads, do you, lass?'

He could sense her reluctance and prompted her further. 'Go on, tell me the truth.'

She hesitated before replying. 'Tom, I've signed the pledge. You know I don't like you drinking, but it's not really a wife's place to tell her husband what to do, and you are on holiday, my love. It's just that Betty Cropper was saying there was some kind of fight in the Foxhall last night.'

Tom shook his head. 'It wasn't a fight, just some young lad getting a bit mouthy with Bob. Not showing him the respect an old soldier deserves. These kids think they're men but they haven't lived. They haven't seen what we've seen. I just put the lad back in his place. It was all over before it began.'

'Oh, Tom, I'd have thought you'd seen enough violence to last a lifetime.'

He took a few silent breaths and then the grin returned to his face. 'Bob and the others will do just fine without me. Why don't you and I do the Tower Ballroom tonight? If you feel up to it.'

'Tom, you hate dancing.'

'Nay, lass. You're confusing me with another Tom Haworth. I love dancing.'

The resort's tower wore a fresh coat of thick dark-red paint in an effort to protect its recently renewed steel from the corrosive effects of sea salt and spray. It had been opened some 30 years previously, five years after Gustave Eiffel's Parisian landmark. It was only half the height of its inspiration, and to some eyes, looked stunted and graceless in comparison, but it was the wonder of northern England and the pride of Blackpool. Whilst the tower in Paris had been erected to demonstrate French engineering supremacy on the centennial of the Revolution, its Lancashire cousin had a strictly commercial intent. The legs of the Eiffel Tower spread wide in an elegant quartet of open arches. In Blackpool they were hidden within a huge red-brick temple of pleasure, a building ornamented with fine terra cotta detailing and crowned by tall cupolas. A vast sign across its doorway proclaimed it 'The Wonderland of the World', and its attractions included a grotto-like aquarium; a menagerie with lions, tigers and polar bears; roof gardens (constructed after the style of the Crystal Palace); and an oriental village. The outline of the Tower's great steel legs was revealed in the jewel-like circus, decorated to resemble a Moroccan sultan's palace and set centrally between them. Its party piece came at the climax of every performance when powerful hydraulics sank the ring and flooded it with seawater, allowing spectacles such as performing seals bobbing and diving in their natural element.

Despite such competition, the crowning glory of the Tower complex was its magnificent ballroom. Designed in neo-Baroque excess by the great theatre architect Frank Matcham, it had elaborate gilded scroll work and mouldings, 16 crystal chandeliers, two tiers of balconies, and ceiling murals depicting fantastic scenes set amongst the clouds. Its sprung floor was tiled with over 30,000 blocks of mahogany, oak and walnut, formed into intricate geometric patterns and onto which hundreds of couples would squeeze every night.

Tom and Clara arrived early enough to find a seat only a little way back from the dance floor. To those accustomed to the utilitarian interiors of the factory or mill, it felt like they were sitting in a palace. It was impossible for them to imagine anywhere more opulent or luxurious; no king or queen could live in greater splendour.

The musicians on the high stage that occupied one end of the room had begun playing, and several couples were already gliding about in expert unison.

Tom put his mouth to his wife's ear. 'This lot are pretty good. When I said I loved dancing, that didn't necessarily mean I could remember any steps.'

Clara laughed and gave him a playful shove. 'I seem to recall you remembered how to waltz at my brother's wedding. Well after a fashion, anyway. I'm happy just sitting here, watching and listening. We'll see how you feel when they play a waltz. If you're feeling brave, we'll get up and give it a try.'

'I'm a brave man, lass. Have I never told you that?' said Tom cheerfully but without conviction.

The band picked up a new tune and Clara confirmed that this was, indeed, a waltz. Most of the couples still sitting at the tables got up and made their way onto the floor. Bolstered by the promise of concealment amongst the throng, Tom led Clara to join them. After a faltering start, they were soon spinning slowly around in time to the music. Clara was somewhat surprised by her husband's new found talent. They were repeating the same basic steps without the embellishments of the more accomplished dancers, but he was moving with an easy rhythm and grace. At her brother's wedding he'd been clumsy and trodden on her toes more than once. Perhaps that was because of the quantity of beer he had consumed that day? Maybe he'd always been able to dance?

They sat out the next few numbers and then a new tune started and Clara announced, 'We can do a one-step to this. Have you ever done a one-step? It's a bit old-fashioned now, but you can dance it to lots of things. We can pretend it's a foxtrot.'

'I've never done a one-step, but I like the sound of it. One step is about my limit. If we hide in the middle, you can try to teach me. Depends if you're feeling brave now.'

Tom quickly mastered the rudiments, and his repertoire of two dances was enough to keep them entertained until his old leg wound started to complain and they decided to call it a night.

They were both tired and happy when they returned to the boarding house and climbed into bed. Clara fell asleep almost immediately, but Tom lay on his pillow looking at her face in the dim light and listening to her soft breathing. The alien voice in his head told him that sleep would take her from him and he made a conscious effort to stay awake, but eventually his eyes closed and his mind drifted away.

Chapter sixteen

I *can see the grey-brown shadow of the pier floating and swaying on the mirrored sea. I can feel the cool water caressing my feet and the sand sinking and sucking at my toes. I turn and there is a shining black rampart defending the land and beyond and above it a lattice of maroon thrusting up into the blue, cloudless sky.*

And on the pale-gold sand I see him, brave and strong, wearing that hat that suited him so much, his impassive face broken for once by the handsomest of smiles.

I feel the gentle rocking of a boat that is not a boat, and I look down like a bird over lines of black slate roofs and a funnel of bright steel railway tracks leading from long, straight canopies leaking smoke and steam. And he is there also, gazing towards me not the view.

The image changes again to one of cream, green, blue, grey, red and gold. Most of all, gold. The colours spin as I turn round and round in his arms.

That was her happiest day. Searching through her memories, those which are left to me, I'm sure of it: the promise of new life, the simple pleasures of music and dance, the warmth of sunlight and affection.

I, more than anyone, know that she always held onto the good times rather than the bad, and that she always saw the best in people. Even so, I know he was different that day. He showed a face she had barely seen before. It was as if he was guided by a different conscience, a different soul.

As if he, too, had a visitor.

Chapter seventeen

He was woken by the distant barking of a dog. It was dark and all he could see was a grey wall, a foot or so from his face. He slowly slid his hand across the bed behind him, but it reached the cold edge unopposed. He was alone. He rolled over and the red bars of the alarm said 6:35. He lay there watching the figures progress until 7:14 became 7:15 and it squealed another Monday morning into existence.

He washed and dressed, and then as he walked around his small flat, he noticed disarray and untidiness. Anyone else would have seen rooms that were simply lived in, but Tom saw objects that were not in their allotted place. His laptop was precariously balanced on the edge of the coffee table; the TV remote was nowhere to be seen, and a newspaper was open on the floor. He wondered briefly if his wife had come back and then remembered she didn't have a key. Even so, he smiled at the fanciful thought of her sneaking in, moving things around to upset him and then sneaking out again. She no longer loved him but not even Amanda could be so petty.

No, no-one else ever came into the flat but him. For once in his life he hadn't put things away. He decided it really didn't matter and left for work.

His morning was allotted to admin and he stole a few minutes to search the Internet. He had been to Blackpool a couple of times as a boy before cheap packages to Spain guaranteed the family a sunnier alternative. He knew the Tower, of course, but there was nothing like the giant Ferris wheel that he could remember. Googling *Blackpool big wheel* threw up some pictures of a modern wheel on

Central Pier, but it was a poor imitation of the structure he and Clara had ridden. What he was looking for closely resembled the great wheel in Vienna. It was a city he'd never visited, but he was something a film buff and the wheel had been a backdrop in one of the Timothy Dalton Bonds and, most famously, in *The Third Man*. Orson Welles stood next to it as he delivered his famous line that warfare, terror and bloodshed in Italy under the Borgias produced the Renaissance, whereas five hundred years of Swiss brotherly love and democracy resulted in the cuckoo clock. Tom began to doubt himself. Were iconic images infiltrating and corrupting his dreams? Had his mind relocated an Austrian landmark to northern England? Was this evidence that everything was being manufactured by his own imagination?

And then he found it: a grainy black-and-white photograph of Blackpool Tower in the 1920s, taken from the sea. Behind it was a giant Ferris wheel with gondolas like railway carriages. The text explained it had been modelled after one built for the Chicago Exposition in 1893. A British engineer had acquired the European rights to the patent and built wheels in London, Paris, Vienna and Blackpool. Only the Viennese Riesenrad still stood, Blackpool's Big Wheel being demolished in 1928.

Once again Tom had convinced himself of his ability to travel back into his grandfather's past. For the first time, however, the memory had been a happy one. And it had not been triggered by alcohol; abstinence or otherwise did not offer him control.

The rotas had been changed, and Carl and Tom no longer worked on the same classes. They kept their distance, and when they did cross paths, limited their interaction to the briefest of acknowledgements. Tom wondered whether he should try to build bridges. After all, Carl had been right about one thing. What they taught was, to a large extent, a pointless tick in an EU box. The bus drivers were bored and disinterested. At best, they were grateful for a break from a life behind a perspex screen and the abusive public it shielded them from. Tom had known it all along, of course. But it had been easier to pretend, to give value to his daily drudge, easier than facing up to the challenge and effort of finding something more worthwhile.

He carried on regardless, and each day passed without him succumbing to the temptation of drink. He slept badly, lying awake each night wondering where his dreams might take him but always woke with a mind empty of images of the past. He knew alcohol would help him sleep, but he still suspected a connection between it and his grandfather's more painful memories and that proved another convincing argument for sobriety.

Some 10 days since he dreamt of the holiday with Clara, he found himself beginning to sneeze at work. At first he thought it might be dust or some other allergen, but then his voice became croaky and his head began to ache. He decided one of the drivers must have passed on a cold, probably acquired from some snot-nosed child on the bus to school. Tom taught his class as best he could, but resisted the temptation to go back to his desk and left for home more promptly than usual. He'd never had any time off sick at Mills, and despite his growing disillusionment, he still felt it was an important point of principle. Some of his colleagues, including Carl, seemed to think they had an annual quota of sick days over and above their leave allowance, but only the most debilitating illness would keep Tom from dragging himself into the office. He wasn't sure if he'd been instilled with a northern Protestant work ethic or whether he was simply a mug. In the past, he'd felt slightly guilty when Carl had given him a hard time for coming into work whilst 'infectious', but Tom suspected he would be spared the hard time, if not the guilt, from now on.

He could face nothing more than a tin of soup for dinner and went to bed early, in the hope of sleeping it off or at least being more rested for the day ahead. Tired and weakened by the virus, he slipped into unconsciousness within minutes of his head touching the pillow.

Chapter eighteen

There was a painfully familiar throbbing in his temple. He pushed it away as his senses became dominated by the smells and sounds of a summer morning. Through half-open eyes he saw bright sunlight filtering through the fabric of drawn curtains, which gently swayed over an open window. Flecks of dust floated on the air and a fly buzzed intermittently and without urgency. Outside, he could faintly hear two voices exchanging the time time of day.

He was lying in an iron-framed bed, wider than his own, but narrower than the double he had previously shared with Amanda. His hand slid across and felt a warm hollow next to him. A soft, feminine aroma floated up from the bedclothes before being lost in the stale fumes of his own exhaled breath.

He lifted himself up onto his pillow and looked around the room. The walls were covered with a pale striped paper and there was small fireplace with a iron cowl in the centre of the far wall. A dark painted wardrobe sat on one side, a mismatched chest of drawers on the other. The curtains had a floral pattern and covered a small sash window whose frame formed a billowing shadow against them.

He looked into his mind and found contentment. He was lying in his own bed in his small terraced house in Burnley. The house he shared with Clara. It was her body that had formed the indentation next to him. There were no children yet, but they were together and happy. Surely they were happy? He found himself questioning the assertion as if there was an impediment lying just beyond his grasp.

The bedroom door was slightly ajar and through the narrow gap he began to hear sounds, indistinct at first but soon unmistakable. They provided the answer.

Part of him wanted to close his eyes, to go to sleep and leave this day behind, but Tom Haworth, the one-time soldier, the young man who had been afraid of nothing, climbed out of bed and made his way down the stairs.

She was in the back parlour, sat at the heavy wooden table, hunched forward with her face buried in her hands. She was sobbing. Though he was bare-footed and entered the room noiselessly, she became aware of his presence and looked up.

Her eyes were reddened by tears and the left side of her face was badly bruised. In unison, the two voices in Tom's head howled in shame. He sank down into the chair opposite her; his head dropped and he stared at the table, not knowing what to say or do. The previous night, his return from the pub, the argument of his making, all came back to him with sharp, painful clarity. He saw himself looking down from Thwaite Pike all those years ago, full of courage and optimism, and wondered how a man could fall so far.

Clara spoke first. 'I'm scared, Tom. You frighten me. I don't know what to do. You're my husband and I can't escape. I know you saw terrible things in the war; I know I lost the baby, but I can't live like this. I hate your drinking. I've asked you so many times to stop or at least slow down, but you're a man, you do what you want. But you're getting drunk more and more. And it makes you so angry. Last night... I never thought it would come to this. Have you seen my face? I can't go to church looking like this.'

Tom's gaze remained fixed on the grain of the table's oak planks. After a long silence he looked up and began to beg. 'I'll sign the pledge, lass. It's what you've always wanted. I'll sign the pledge and give up the drink for good. I'll change. I have to change. This is not the man I ever saw myself becoming. I can't be this man.'

She said nothing in reply but doubt was written on her face.

He continued his pleading. 'We'll go up to the village and see the minister this afternoon, after the service is over. He'll sort out the formalities; we'll do it properly. I'll swear an oath of abstinence in front of him and holy God.'

'You don't believe in God, Tom. Not anymore, not since you were in France.'

'Then I'll swear it in front of you. Trust me, Clara. Inside me there's still the man you once loved, the man of strength you once admired. There's enough of him left to make this happen. We can start again. I love you, Clara.'

Her look of doubt receded and was replaced by the faintest suggestion of hope. 'You know, you've only ever told me that twice before.' She stared into his eyes as if searching for that hidden man within. 'Alright, Tom. I have to trust you. I have no choice. We'll go and see the minister.'

They climbed off the bus at the old toll booth on the brow of the hill where the road forked. The bus went left, but the right turn led towards the village. They were half a mile above the reservoir and strode downhill at a healthy pace. Clara wore her hat low over her face in a largely successful attempt to conceal the deepening blackness of the bruising. They passed a few people whom they knew but exchanged only cursory greetings and maintained their progress unchecked. They reached the church in a little over twenty minutes, by which time it was just after 2:00 pm. The grounds seemed deserted, but they knew Percy Chambers was a man of strict habit and would be in his office at the rear of the building.

As they walked down the narrow side path, they met Ann Lord pushing her husband in a cane framed wheelchair. Bill's body looked frail and emaciated. The right side of his head was scarred by burns and empty trouser legs hung over the front of the chair. He stared up at Tom with clear, undisguised hatred. Ann's expression was harder to read; she'd scanned Clara's face and something approaching a smirk flickered across her lips. Tom thought he recognised *schadenfreude*; he knew it meant pleasure derived from another's misfortune but couldn't quite place where he'd learnt such a strange, foreign word.

'Bill, how are you?' he asked.

'How do you think? How does it look?' snarled the man who had once been his best friend.

'I tried to come and see you in the hospital, but they said, well... They said you didn't want me there.'

'It was bad enough Ann here having to visit me. Acting out the charade of the loving, devoted wife. The truth is, you're just waiting for me to die aren't you, my love? Hoping your looks don't desert you first. You don't want to get fat and ugly like your mother. Well, not until you've ensnared a proper husband, one who isn't a useless cripple.'

Ann snapped down at him, 'That's enough, Bill. Wait till I get you home!'

She then addressed the other couple as she bulldozed them out of the way with the chair. 'If you don't mind, we need to get past. We're in a hurry. By the state of Clara's face it looks like you have urgent business with the minister yourselves. Somebody needs some guidance I expect. Isn't that right, Tom?'

Tom and Clara were left looking at each other dispiritedly. Only Clara spoke. 'We just need to be thankful we're not in their shoes. We can get through this, Tom.'

Percy Franklin Chambers made no attempt to hide his anger. His Midlands accent became more pronounced as he expressed his indignation at what Tom had done to his wife. He denounced it as the lowest form of cowardice and declared Tom's war service an irrelevance: a man's true character was revealed through his treatment of people weaker than himself. Tom sensed the tirade was amplified by the feelings the minister once held for Clara, but he knew it was deserved and sat in compliant silence.

Clara wasn't sure her husband would accept such quasi-parental scolding indefinitely and raised her left hand to stop the reddening cleric in mid flow.

'Percy, please. Tom knows he's done wrong. He's full of remorse, trust me. It's the drink. You know what it can do to a man. You've always told us; you've always preached against it. He sees it now; he wants to sign the pledge. We're going to start again. Please help us.'

The minister visibly calmed and a more natural colour returned to his face. He slowly exhaled. 'Yes, of course. It just a crying shame someone didn't listen to me when he was younger. Still...' He paused while he searched for an appropriate quotation. '"If your brother sins, rebuke him, and if he repents forgive him." We'll take the oath together. One more convert, only a few more million to go before we rid this land of the evil of alcohol. If only our government had the courage to introduce prohibition like their American counterparts.'

That night as they lay in bed, she looked at her husband's profile and stretched over to kiss his forehead. 'It's going to be alright, isn't it?

Tom nodded. 'I'll make sure it's alright.'

He knew the sacrifice would challenge him, but he had the strength to carry it through. He had given his word and it would not be broken. He would be sober, forever. He would regain his self-respect and, if at all possible, the love of his wife.

Chapter nineteen

He woke naturally and lifted himself sharply onto his elbow when he saw the time. It was 8:47. He was never late for work, ill or not. He threw back the duvet and then sank back down onto his pillow. Two sets of memories from the previous day slowly intermingled. The more insistent had a remorseful man swearing on a bible in a Pennine church, but there was another self in a different setting that lingered fuzzily in the background. That picture suddenly emerged like the face in a misted mirror swept clear by a hand. He saw himself in Jimmy Mills' office, handing in his resignation. Jimmy was telling him to clear his desk and that he didn't need to work out his notice.

Tom wasn't late. He didn't have a job to go to.

He lay back trying to understand what could have made him act so rashly. He only had a cold; he hadn't been suffering from delirium. It was true that the job was unfulfilling and meaningless, but so were a lot of jobs. He still had money in the bank from his share of the sale of the house. That, however, was meant for a deposit on somewhere new, not to be squandered on a whim. He'd eaten into it enough when he'd lost his position at the bank.

And then his analysis changed. It hadn't been a whim; for once in his life he had been decisive. The job was stifling him. He was capable of better and could afford to take time out to find something more rewarding and worthwhile.

He briefly felt some guilt over Jimmy. After all, his boss had stood up for him over the incident with Carl Singleton. Then he remembered a snippet of conversation from Jimmy's mouth, 'This is probably for the best. Carl's causing a bit of disquiet around the office.' Tom sensed that yesterday he didn't care about anyone else: he was just putting himself first. But today it mattered that he wasn't letting Jimmy down.

Tom spent the day on job websites, trying to understand the options available to someone with a background in statistics. He didn't want to return to the world of banking with its obsessive focus on money and profit. Roles like biomedical research were far too specialised. As always, nearly every job called for years of experience in a specific industry or role. There were a few opportunities in the charity and education sectors for which he felt qualified, but they were all outside London. He hadn't been expecting to find the answer immediately, so he felt reassured that he was, at least, employable. How many people would be applying for each position and whether he'd even get as far as an interview were different questions. Even so, he decided he needed to spend a little time thinking about what was important to him and what he was looking for. Moving out of London, for example, would be a hassle, but it would save money in the long-term, and he no longer had any real ties. He had finally accepted that Amanda and he were finished.

Concentrating on his employment situation had taken his mind off the other drama he had been walking in and out of like an actor in a minor role. When he turned his attention away from his laptop, that other Tom came back centre stage.

He began to wonder which of them had taken the oath of abstinence that day. It had the feel of a complex philosophical paradox, but he determined that he, for certain, would be bound by it. He had broken his share of promises over the years; he would not break this one. He had given his solemn word to someone who had become the most important person in his life, despite not being in his life at all.

Tom's cold had seemed past it worst, but after a long day concentrating on job descriptions and qualification requirements, it re-announced itself in an aching back and tired eyes. Tom climbed into bed, and for once, was not overwhelmed by questions. He sensed an order creeping into his life and was swiftly consumed by sleep.

Chapter twenty

He lay in the iron-framed bedstead he had woken in two days previously. Was it two days, one day or a lifetime ago?

He had little time to ponder on his surroundings. Clara strode in and spoke firmly.

'Come on, Tom! Out of bed. We don't want to miss the bus and end up late. I won't be running down that hill you know.'

She wore a cream cotton nightdress which hung over the large bulge at her middle like a pelmet on a lamp. She was heavily pregnant.

'Are you sure you want to come, lass? The baby's due in a few weeks and no-one will blame you for missing the funeral. It'll be a sad affair, one way or another. You've not been that well. It would be best if you stayed at home.'

'If it was just the funeral I would, but I want to see my brother and Mary. I know what it's like to lose a baby. I've made up my mind. I'm coming.'

The single-decker Leyland struggled noisily as it negotiated the sharp bends of the narrow road climbing up into the hills. The vibration made Clara feel slightly nauseous and Tom watched the expression on her face with discomfort. When they reached the derelict toll booth, the driver pulled over and waited patiently as Tom helped his wife down off the bus. The sky was threateningly dark, and with little cover on the way, Tom hoped the clouds would hold on to their burden long enough for them to reach the sanctuary of the church.

As they walked slowly and carefully down the road, his concern for her was balanced by the knowledge he had become the decent, reliable husband she deserved. He had kept to his pledge, and the memory of that dark night of bullying violence towards her had become slightly less painful. He had avoided the urge to bury the shame away and held it close in case temptation crept up on him unawares. Evenings previously spent in the pub were now occupied tinkering with a homemade crystal set radio, trying to tune in to broadcasts from the BBC's Manchester transmitter. For her part, Clara was relieved to be living without fear and was gratified to see her husband regain his self-esteem. Occasionally she hoped for his warm, gentler side to revisit, but she contented herself that he was, once more, the strong, proud man she had married.

When they eventually reached the church, there was a small crowd of people standing outside ignoring the intermittent spits of light rain. Martha Lord was greeting people with the pained smile of a grieving mother. Tom and Clara waited their turn and then Clara gave her a gentle hug while Tom nodded his head respectfully.

Tom had never known her to look youthful, but the last few years had been hard on Martha. She had lost weight about her face and looked as if the next funeral she would attend might be her own. Her words were punctuated by the heavy wheeze of someone whose lungs had been irreparably damaged by too many years inhaling cotton dust in a humid throstle room. Nonetheless, she spoke with a motherly concern for the young couple.

'Clara, you shouldn't have come in your condition, but it's lovely to see you. You're looking so well, my dear. I'm sure things will turn out grand this time. And, Tom, I wanted to say how sorry I am for how our Bill treated you. He was so... so bitter. I don't know why he blamed you. You were such good friends when you were young 'uns. Up and down them hills, paddling in the brook. They were such happy times. Can you forgive him, lad?'

'There's nothing to forgive, Mrs Lord. His injuries were so awful it would make any man bitter. At least he's not suffering any longer.'

'Aye, lad, it's a blessing. I'll miss him terribly, but it's a blessing.'

Her tone hardened. 'And that wife of his, I'm sure it's a blessing for her also.'

On cue, Ann Lord appeared at her side. She was wearing a new black dress bought specially for the funeral. It was simple but fashionable, and the colour complimented her dark features such that Tom wondered if he'd ever seen her look so beautiful. Her eyes seemed to sparkle beguilingly in betrayal of the expressionless line of her mouth. She gave Clara only the most cursory recognition and then focussed on Tom like a cat sizing up a mouse.

'Tom, I'm glad you and Clara could come. It's a sad day but it's for the best you know. He didn't want go on living like that. I'm sure you understand, Tom. Don't you?'

'Yes, I understand, lass. I wouldn't have changed places with him for anything.'

'Wouldn't you, Tom?'

Tom felt uncomfortable under Ann's confusing stare. 'No. Look, there'll be lots of folk who want to express their condolences. We don't want to keep you. Clara and I will head inside now. We'll see you after the service.'

He quickly led his wife through the heavy wooden door of the church. Sitting alone towards the back with his head bowed was Clara's brother, Harold.

Clara squeezed next to him and took his hands in hers.

'Harry, how are you? How's Mary?'

'She couldn't face coming today. You understand. She's still a bit weak, to be honest, and losing the baby's broken her heart.'

'Oh, Harry, I know it seems like the world's come to an end, but you'll both get over it. You can try again.

Look at Tom and me. Well, look at me anyway.' She put a hand on her bump and smiled expectantly at her brother.

He looked down at his feet before replying, 'The doctor doesn't hold out much hope of us having another, I'm afraid.'

The church slowly filled with solemn-faced mourners. The background mumbling of whispered conversation was immediately silenced when the minister took his place at the simple lectern. His eulogy spoke of Bill Lord's happy childhood in the village, his youthful good looks and his heroism in the Great War. Despite his crippling wounds, he was a fine husband, a stalwart friend and a dutiful son. God had tested him with great suffering, but he had borne it with fortitude and courage. All along, he had trusted in Jesus as his Saviour and had now risen to a perpetual afterlife in Heaven above.

Percy Chambers paused and looked around his church, trying to catch the eye of everyone present. Finally, his gaze rested on a tearful Martha Lord in the front row. He raised his voice over the heavy rain that had suddenly begun hammering against the roof.

'And there he will be whole again, walking on his own two legs, with Jesus at his side. I believe that with all my heart.'

The final hymn was *Abide with Me* and it was rendered in good voice with scant need for the church's well-thumbed hymn books. By the last chorus the heavens had relented, and there was just a fine drizzle when the congregation filed out to the muddy graveside. Bill's family had one of the original plots in the lower graveyard close by the church door. Tom insisted Clara stay inside the doorway rather than risk the cold and damp.

By the amen of the final prayer, the sky had brightened and hints of blue leached through thinning white clouds. Tom and Harold stood side by side; Clara came out and took her brother's arm before addressing them both.

'Harry, I'd like to go up and see Mum and Dad's grave. It might do you good to spend a few quiet moments with them. Tom, will you come too? A strong man on each arm will get me up that hill in no time.'

Tom looked over to the steep path that climbed between the trees to the upper graveyard. Its drenched grey-black stones began to shine as the sun broke through and rivulets of water ran down the shallow guttering on each side. Not for the first time, he felt a sense of foreboding, as if there was something of unremitting sorrow waiting for him at the top of the slope, something he could not bear to face. He did not believe in ghosts. The bones of the dead held no fear for him, but he found himself fixed by inexplicable dread and his weaker side held sway.

'Clara, would you forgive me if I don't? I don't know why, but I really can't face going up there today.'

She frowned, somewhat bemused that he should refuse such a simple request, but then the smile reappeared on her face. 'Don't worry. Harry and I will be fine. It's only like climbing a couple of flights of stairs. I'm not an invalid. We'll be back soon.'

Brother and sister began ascending slowly. Tom briefly watched and then turned away when Ann Lord approached him.

'Thanks again for coming, Tom. It was a nice service, don't you think? The minister said all the right things. He painted Bill in a good light, which is the way it should be.'

'You're right, but I always hate funerals I'm afraid, Ann. When the time comes, I'm tempted to say that I don't want one myself, though I don't know if you'd get away with such a thing. So, what do you plan to do now? Will you stay in the village?'

He had been struggling for conversation and quickly realised the question could be taken as disrespectful. He tried to correct himself. 'Forgive me, I'm forgetting myself. A widow needs time to grieve for her husband,

and a proper period of mourning needs to be observed. You're still young enough to sort yourself out when the time's right.'

'Sort myself out?' There was a playful tone in Ann's voice. 'All the good men were either killed in the war or are already spoken for. I don't know what—'

There was a scream.

Tom span round towards it. Clara was tumbling down the near vertical bank between the upper and lower graveyards. Harold was frantically scrambling down after her. Tom raced over to try to break her fall, but by the time he reached her she was lying on the grass below. He collapsed on his knees beside her and grasped her hand.

'Clara, are you alright? Clara, tell me you feel alright!'

There was a dazed expression on her face.

'Oh, Tom, what have I done? That was clumsy of me.'

Her hands felt for her stomach and her face began to shift into a mask of pain. For the briefest flash, Tom was taken back to Bill's face on that hideous day in the trenches.

Clara cried out, 'Oh, Tom, it hurts! What have I done?' Panic entered her voice.

'What have I done? Oh, the baby! I'm so sorry, Tom. Forgive me. Oh, Tom! It hurts; I can't bear it.'

Tom felt powerless. All he could do was stroke her hair and mutter empty reassurances. 'You've just had a bit of a knock, that's all. You're bit a shaken up. Everything will be alright, trust me.'

Behind him, he heard Percy Chambers take control. 'Freddie! Come here, boy!'

A skinny youngster of fifteen shot over.

'Now then, son, get on that bike of yours and get down to Doctor Morley's as fast as you can. Tell him Mrs Haworth's baby's nearly due and she's had a bad fall. She's in a lot of pain. Now go!'

The minister turned his attention to Harold Hargreaves, who was standing covered in mud and in a state of shock as he looked down over his sister and Tom. 'Harold, pull yourself together, lad. Help your brother-in-law carry Clara into my house. Gently now.'

A stout elderly woman came over and spoke calmly to the minister whose hands were beginning to shake perceptibly. 'I've helped my share of mothers bring babies into this world. I'd better go with her too.'

'Thank you, Mrs Patchett. I'd be very grateful. I just hope the doctor gets here soon. This is just too awful. Mrs Haworth is a very dear to… to us all.'

Tom didn't know how much time had passed since they'd carried Clara into the large, comfortable room at the front of the minister's house. She'd been almost delirious with pain, and his efforts at comforting her had brought her no relief. When the doctor had finally arrived, Tom had been banished to the back kitchen.

There was now only the occasional sound of muffled words coming from the other room. The light was beginning to fade and the lamps had not been lit. Harold was still there, pacing back and forth incessantly. Tom sat motionless at the heavy wooden table with his head in his hands. Despite his loss of faith, he was praying for the first time since he'd come home from the trenches, offering God any exchange, any price for Clara to be safe, for her ordeal to end. He was even willing to give Him the baby they'd wanted for so long.

Harold broke the silence.

'It's all my fault. I should have realised how slippy it were. I should have held on to her properly. What sort of brother am I?'

Tom continued staring at the table but shook his head. 'Nay, Harry. I told you earlier. I'm to blame. She asked me to come with you and I said no. I don't understand why, but I said no. It was unforgivable. There's something in me sometimes that I don't understand. I was frightened of the graveyard. Can you believe that?

When I was younger, I used to think I was afraid of nothing. And now I'm scared of shadows. Me mum, God bless her, always warned me about running away from things. She was right. Look where it's led me. Look what I've done to Clara.'

He looked up and beckoned Harold over. Tom gripped his brother-in-law's forearm and shook it reassuringly before correcting himself. 'Listen to us both. Self-pity and blame aren't going to do anybody any good. You'd better get home to your Mary. She'll be worried sick. There's not a lot you can do here.'

'I don't know what to say to her, Tom. She's already so upset about losing her own baby. If Clara loses hers it will break my Mary's heart.'

'That's the reason you have to be with her. Don't you start running away from things too. Now, put your coat on—'

The door between the two rooms opened.

Standing in the doorway was a short, thin man of about sixty with a balding head and rheumy, pale eyes. His expression was solemn.

'Doctor, how is she?' burst out Tom. 'Has she lost the baby?'

'Mr Haworth,' began the doctor carefully, 'please prepare yourself. I have something very difficult to tell you—'

Tom shot upright in bed. The bars of the clock read 03:26. He was panting short, urgent breaths; his heart was hammering against his ribs and his back was drenched in sweat. He was engulfed with a pulsing terror which slowly ebbed as it was overtaken by the shame of craven betrayal. His feeble mind had surrendered. Like a soldier deserting under fire, it had woken him rather than face the horror that was unfolding in his dream. He pulled his knees to his chest and his whole body winced in disgrace. Would his cowardice never cease? He forced himself to lie down again, clamped shut his eyes and desperately tried to will himself back to sleep. Once again, he begged a God he didn't believe in, begged to be sent back, but He was not listening.

After several minutes, Tom accepted the futility of his efforts, opened his eyes and stared up a dark ceiling lit only by the faint red glow from the clock. Slowly, the colour began to awake a different image, which formed in his mind from somewhere deep in his buried memories.

He was a boy, five years old at most. He was climbing out of a car. He recognised it. It was the battered old Hillman his father had kept for years and would later embarrass Tom when his school friends were collected in newer, smarter vehicles.

The sun was shining and he was standing in a small car park covered with warm yellow gravel. He had the sense of it crunching as he walked, but the unfolding narrative was silent and his steps made no sound. Standing next to him was a tall man with jet-black wavy hair. Tom caught a vague aroma of tobacco and Brylcreem. A packet of cigarettes appeared in the man's palm; he took one out and tapped it against the face of the pack.

Tom found himself doubting the last picture. It felt like an interloper, a standard paragraph inserted into the wrong document. It was a gesture he'd seen so many times, but somehow it didn't belong here.

His credence returned as he saw himself reach up and take the man's hand. Tom felt the contact envelope him in a blanket of safety and certainty. He was an innocent who was guaranteed forgiveness for any crime. The man provided protection from anything and everything. In five year-old Tom's eyes, he was the bravest, the cleverest, and without question, the handsomest man in the world. He was wearing fawn trousers, a plain white collared shirt and a bright red v-necked sweater.

Tom and his father walked across the car park and began climbing a steep path of grey-black stone. Leafy branches hung over them and their feet stepped through a pattern of shade and light that swayed with the gentle breeze. When they reached the top there was a small field covered with several lines of gravestones. The grass was a sharp, shining green and the monuments, a uniform, weathered grey. Some were tall and ornate, but many were simple, small blocks laying on the ground. Tom saw himself standing in front of one stone that seemed different to the others. It was shiny and black with gold lettering. It stood taller than Tom and as he looked up he saw his father's lips moving, but the words were silent.

Tom's eyes watched his own perfect, young finger reach out and begin tracing the engraved letters. He could see they were in clear, legible capitals, but no matter how hard he tried, they seemed as indecipherable as Chinese pictograms.

Tom lay on his bed and the image of the gravestone began to fade. He was left with nothing except the indistinct shadows of night, but in that darkness, it seemed clear this hidden childhood memory had inspired the sense of foreboding whenever he neared the graveyard in his dreams.

But whose name was written in gold on the black marble stone? Was it Clara's? Was that what he had been so afraid of finding? If so, he, and she, were victim to a cruel, twisted temporal paradox. The grave wouldn't have been there on the damp day of Bill Lord's funeral. How could it be? Clara was alive. Tom could have held tightly on to his pregnant wife as she climbed that lethal slope. There would be no black marble harbinger of death awaiting him.

An overwhelming pall of guilt, grief and senselessness held him motionless until dawn began to leak into the room. With great difficulty he lifted himself from his bed and dressed. He didn't shave and splashed a token gesture of water on his face before making for the hallway. Despite the postman's increasingly late arrival, mail was already lying on the mat. Most of it was brightly coloured and addressed to 'The Occupier', but one letter stood out in a plain white window envelope. Tom distractedly picked it up and put it in his pocket. He slammed the door behind him and hurried down the wakening street. For the first time in months, he didn't stop at the garden gate and double back to check the door was properly shut.

Chapter twenty-one

Tom arrived at the library wishing he'd put on a warmer jacket. There was a persistent wind and it exaggerated the coldness of the morning air. His regret was intensified when he found the entrance locked. He checked his watch and then the library notice board to find the building wouldn't open for another hour. He cursed his own impatient stupidity and made his way back to the high street in search of breakfast. There was a long shelf that formed a narrow table in the cafe window and was the preserve of lone customers such as himself. He perched on a high stool and stared out at the people rushing on their way to work. He envied them their purpose. He was sure they all had certainties in their lives, whereas his own was nothing but confusion and, perhaps, foolishness. His bacon sandwich sat on its plate barely touched, but he managed to drink his coffee whilst he calculated and visualised the steps he would carry out when logged onto the library computer.

Tom had been standing outside for 10 minutes when the grey-haired librarian pulled back the stiff bolts that secured the ancient panelled door. He greeted Tom with a smile.

'Good morning. It's nice to see you again. You're not normally one of our mid-week early birds.'

Tom tried not to look, or sound, manic and agitated. He was not successful as he gabbled a reply, 'Yeh, I'm sort of between jobs at the moment. Look, I know I haven't booked, again, but I wanted to do some more family history stuff. I'm sure I can get back into the website myself, but if I need some guidance would you be able to spare me five minutes or so? I'd really, really appreciate it if you could. Would that be okay, do you think?'

The librarian maintained his steady smile, but there was a slight suggestion of unease in his narrowing eyebrows. 'Yes, of course. I'm sure that'll be okay. Obviously, if we get a rush at the counter I might get tied up...' The smile developed a wry twist as he glanced at a robotic sentinel in the lobby. 'But now they've installed the self-issuing machines, that's not too likely. I must admit I enjoy helping people with family history. It's a bit like solving a crossword or a jigsaw puzzle. A jigsaw where, unfortunately, one or more of the pieces are often missing. Anyway, give me a shout when you need me to come over.'

Tom had to restrain himself from running as he crossed the empty library to the computer desk in the far corner. He was filled with trepidation but knew the question had to be answered. The doubt was becoming unbearable.

The computer's responses seemed even slower than before, and despite his mental rehearsals in the cafe, it took Tom nearly ten minutes to get into the specific database he needed. For some reason the death indexes were split into two, pre and post 1916. He didn't have an exact year, it hadn't appeared in his dream, but he knew it must have been sometime in the late 1920s so chose the later set of records.

He typed in *Clara Haworth* and only five results were listed down the screen. He discounted the two registered in Nottingham and Liverpool and focussed on the others which were all in the Burnley area. One Clara Haworth was 50 in 1927, far too old, but the others were 32 in 1929 and 71 in 1968. Frustratingly, both ages seemed to fit. He searched deeper, but couldn't find anything to clarify which Clara was his.

He leant back in his chair and looked around the library. There was only one other customer, sitting in a easy chair reading the Daily Mail, and the two members of staff who were taking books out of a large cardboard box at the counter. Tom resisted the temptation to shout and was about to stand when grey-haired librarian looked up and saw him. Tom raised his hand like a schoolboy in class, and the librarian nodded in acknowledgement.

He walked over slowly and sat next to Tom at the desk.

Tom immediately began to babble again. 'I'm stuck. I can't get any further. I need to see more than this. I can't tell which of these two deaths is for the person I'm looking for. I think I need to see the... What do you call them? The certificates. I mean, the death certificates for these records. I've seen my mum and dad's; there's much more information, things like the informant and the exact place of death. I think that would tell me what I need to know. I hope so anyway. But they don't seem to be here. The death certificates. I've clicked on everything and just keep going round in circles.'

'Okay, slow down just a bit' said the librarian. 'In England and Wales, death certificates aren't online. All we have access to are indexes. They give you the basic information, but the detailed certificates have to be ordered from the General Register Office in Southport. There's a charge and they can take a week or so to come though. Your other option is to go to local register office. Would that be nearby?' He looked at the screen. 'No, that's Lancashire, isn't it? I think you'd probably have to go all the way up to Preston. From memory that's the county town.'

Tom looked dejected. He wanted the answer there and then. His brooding was interrupted by the sound of a raised voice from the direction of the counter. The librarian looked round and Tom spoke quickly to regain his attention.

'So how do I go about ordering a certificate from the... Did you say *General* Register Office in Southport?'

'Yes. Erm...' The librarian started to stand. 'Just go to their website; it's all pretty self-explanatory. You'll need the volume and page number from the index entry. And of course, your credit card. Look, I'm sorry, Mr Wilson is in again and causing trouble. He's one of our regulars, if you know what I mean. I'd better go over and help calm him down.'

Despite the distracting argument from across the room, Tom managed to order the two certificates before the computer decided his hour of allowed time had expired and logged him off. The library had become quiet again. Mr Wilson had departed, but only after the librarians had been forced to summon the police. They were now discussing the disturbance with a Community Support Officer who had belatedly arrived.

Tom had written the certificate volume and page numbers on the back of the letter he'd put in his pocket when he'd left the flat. He sat back in his chair, flipped over the envelope, considered it briefly, then tore it open.

Dear Mr Haworth
I would be grateful if you could contact my secretary to arrange an appointment to review your current medication. I would appreciate your prompt attention to this matter.
Yours
Dr D Jacobson.

The note had been pp'd by someone with an indecipherable signature, but presumably the secretary whom Tom was to contact. From previous experience, she was a humourless woman wired for efficiency at the complete expense of charm. She guarded access to her employer like an ill-tempered nightclub bouncer. Tom seldom carried his mobile - it never rang - and decided to phone her as soon as he got home. At least it would get it over with. He went straight back to his flat, and the anticipation of a verbal interrogation partly distracted him from his disappointment at the library.

After two rings a curt voice answered the phone. 'Dr Jacobson's office. Can I help you?'

'Ah, yes, it's Tom Haworth here. The doctor wrote to me asking that I contact you to make an appointment. The only problem is, my health insurance has expired. I'm not employed right now and Dr Jacobson's fees are a bit beyond my means. I'm feeling pretty much okay at the moment and I just wondered if I really needed to come in?'

There was a silence at the other end of the line. Tom was beginning to wonder if they'd been cut off when he received a terse reply. No attempt was made to disguise the irritation in the voice. 'Please hold the line; I'll talk to Dr Jacobson.'

Again the phone went dead. This time it was two minutes before the voice returned. If anything, its tone was even shorter. 'Dr Jacobson says this is important. He has *very* kindly agreed to treat it as a continuation of your last appointment. He can give you ten minutes maximum. You are *exceedingly* fortunate that he is running ahead of schedule today and can slot you in just before we finish this afternoon. You said you weren't working. Please be here at 5:15. Promptly, Mr Haworth, if you please.'

Tom was tempted to be bloody-minded and say 5:15 wasn't convenient, but he resisted. 'That's very good of you. I'll be there on time, don't worry. Thank you very much.'

She hung up. Tom had survived the confrontation and he relaxed, albeit briefly.

He had a couple of hours to kill. He tried to occupy his mind with the mundane repetition of housework and ironing, but the same thoughts kept circulating in his head. Their intensity escalated making him increasingly stressed and agitated. Eventually they followed a different tangent and he thought of his sister and remembered he hadn't replied to her last email. Almost at once, a notion came into his head, a potential clue that he had overlooked. It seemed obvious and he wondered whether some part of his psyche had been blocking it out deliberately.

Hey Sis!

Hope the chipmunks aren't giving you too much bother. (OK, I promise, that's the last time I mention bloody Chipmunks.)
Thanks for sending me the photographs of grandad in uniform. You're right. I do look him him. My hair's starting to thin at an alarming rate, so the resemblance, to his older, balder self, may soon be re-established. Oh god, Sis, I used to worry about silly things like going bald and now they seem so effing unimportant. You said there were some photographs of dads mum at our parents wedding and also one you weren't sure about from when dad was very little. Please can you send those to me as soon as you can. If you could do it today that would be brilliant. Please, Sis, if its at all possble. Sorry to be so pushy, its just that its become really importnat to me. I've not been well, Sis, I didn't want to tell you. Depression, you know. And I was drinking too much. Sarah, I'm an alcoholic. There you go, I've written it in black and white. I am an alcoholic. But I was getting better, honest I was. At least I'm finished with drinking for ever. That's for definite. And I was feeling so much better in myslef. I was feeling good. Until these damn dreams got too much. Ive got to tell someone, Sarah, and your the only one I've got. I've been going back into our grndfathers past. Seeing things that he saw before we were born, before even Dad was born. Ive seen th etrenches of the first world war, Burnley and Rossendale as they used to be. Meeting family I didnt even know existed. I know it sounds barmy but I've got proof. Things Ive been able to verify on the Internet. Grandad's father was called George. How do I know that? But its true. Its on the 1911 census. Grandad's eldest sister was called Ethelina. Now that's not a name you'd make up is it? And there's more. Much too much too much for it to be coincidence. But now its really importnat that I see those photos of dad's mum. I need to

know if I recognise her. Maybe I wont, but until I'm sure its going to eat away at me. Sorry to dump all this on you Sarah. But I've got no one else. Please dont worry. I mean that. When I see those photos I'll be fine. I'll be able to calm down and get myself back on track. So please send them as soon as you can.

Love (and sorry) Tommy xx
PS by the way, I've packed in my job. It was crap anyway.

He had to catch two buses to get to the clinic and could never be sure how long the journey would take. As a result, he'd typed the email in uncharacteristic haste. He'd looked at his watch, panicked, pressed the send button and immediately regretted it. He'd totally lost control of his emotions and said far more than he'd intended. He'd been overcome by the need to share his anxieties with the only person he trusted, and now he'd dragged her into his crazy, impossible world. The one person who had always looked up to him would never respect him again. He thought about typing a second email with the subject line: 'Please don't open my last email', but he looked at his watch and felt there wasn't time. He also knew his sister well enough to know her concern and curiosity would lead her to ignore any such request.

'Oh, shit!' he snapped as he made for the front door.

Chapter twenty-two

Tom arrived at the clinic half an hour early. It was an expansive Victorian mansion, discretely extended with modern wings and sitting in well-manicured grounds that ran down to the river. He stood outside knowing he would not be allowed to see Dr Jacobson one second before the time allotted. The wind was still unpleasantly cold, but the secretary sat at a desk that commanded the waiting room and Tom decided he would rather freeze outside than under her icy and dismissive stare.

Private health insurance was one of the perks of his old job at the bank. In his younger days it had paid for his wisdom teeth to be removed by a Harley Street dentist, but since then his physical health had been good and Dr Jacobson was the only other medical practitioner to have been subsidised by the bank's largesse. His old employer had been keen for Tom to resign rather than having to sack him, and as an inducement, agreed to extend his cover to the end of the financial year. His GP was of the opinion that the clinic offered the finest mental health services in West London and thought they should take advantage whilst the policy was still in force.

The place made Tom feel uncomfortable. It had built a reputation treating the addictions and obsessions of the rich and famous, but its interior seemed rambling, dark and depressing. Presumably, the glitterati were seen in the newly built extensions. The likes of Tom were relegated to the converted corridors and bedrooms of the original house.

At 5:10 pm precisely he entered the small, windowless waiting room. The secretary looked up, acknowledged him with a nod and then returned to the papers on her desk. At 5:15 she clicked a button on her intercom and announced Tom's arrival to Dr Jacobson. A few seconds later, the heavy panelled door behind her opened and a grinning man, who looked to be in his early sixties though still with a heavy mop of salt and pepper hair, ushered Tom in.

The office/consulting room was cramped but had a large sash window with a view over the road at the front of the house. Sight of the river and garden was obviously reserved for people suffering more expensive complaints.

Dr Jacobson began talking with his usual air of confident authority. 'Tom, I'm glad we could get you in so promptly. This won't take us long. How have you been?'

Tom hesitated long enough for a look of disappointment to creep onto Jacobson's face.

'I've been okay, doctor. I've been feeling good really. Definitely kicked the drinking into touch. Apart from that, well, a few ups and downs, but I've been okay.'

'How's the job going?'

'It wasn't right for me. I'm looking for something else.'

The doctor paused and sucked his lower lip. He reminded himself this wasn't a consultation and moved the conversation on. 'In the interests of time, I'll get straight to the matter in hand. Are you still taking the Trempatolam?'

'Yes. You told me not to stop unless I weaned myself off slowly, just like the previous pills. To be honest, I never noticed it doing much for me. I would have stopped but I've had a lot on my mind and it just seemed easier to keep taking it. I had a repeat prescription set up at my local chemist and I guess I was waiting for my GP to ask for a review before I decided what to do.'

The doctor smiled reassuringly. 'As we've discussed before, Tom, modern antidepressants aren't like the "happy pills" of old.' He made the quotation mark gesture with two fingers on each hand. 'Their effects are

119

much more subtle and hard to detect. They will be helping you and you don't realise. That said, they don't always work for everyone. Trempatolam was new; the drug company was very positive about it; it was starting to be very widely prescribed in the US, and I switched you to it because you didn't seem to be responding to the SSRIs I'd normally prescribe.'

The doctor paused once more while he considered his words. 'Unfortunately, we're now getting some worrying reports about Trempatolam. It passed its clinical trials, obviously, but some side effects that had seemed minor became more pronounced when it was released for general use. They are being investigated as we speak, but I've decided to get my own patients off it until we know a bit more. To be honest, I've prescribed it to only you and one other, so I'm not too... Well, I just want to get the two of you off it. The side effects have only been reported in a small minority of cases, nearly all in the States, so it's just a precaution.'

'What sort of side effects are we talking about, doctor?'

'Mood swings, uncharacteristic behaviour patterns, and in some extreme cases, psychotic episodes including hallucinations and delusions. There could be a link to alcohol consumption, they're not sure. Unfortunately, there have been a couple of suicides in America which may, or may not, be attributable to the drug.'

Again the doctor paused and looked carefully at Tom. 'Have you been experiencing any adverse effects? You've definitely been able to stay off the drink?'

Tom was reluctant to reply. He tried to keep his face impassive but sensed it was betraying him. Jacobson maintained his silence and Tom cracked first. He started off hesitantly, then began to accelerate.

'I've lapsed a couple of times, and if I'm honest, I have been having these dreams. This is going to sound mad, seriously mad, but I've been going back into my grandfather's past. It's as if I've been swapping places with him. He's done things, as me, that I would never do, and I've… I've found things out that I couldn't otherwise know. That's the proof. It's all too much for coincidence. I'm almost certain it's a real phenomenon, not any kind of psychotic delusion—'

The doctor interrupted. 'First of all, mad is not a word we use here and secondly, slow down. Please. Now, maybe you could give me an example of these real dreams and the things you couldn't otherwise know?'

'Okay, an easy one. Do you know the big Ferris wheel in Vienna? It was in *The Third Man*. The old film with Orson Welles.'

The doctor nodded slowly. 'The Wiener Riesenrad. My wife's Austrian. I've been on it more than once.'

'Well, did you know there was an almost exact duplicate in Blackpool that was pulled down in the late 1920s? I didn't know until I saw my grandfather on it in one of these dreams. But I've checked it on the Internet and it definitely existed.'

'It does ring a vague bell. Yes, I think I did know about the Big Wheel in Blackpool. Oh, Tom, you could have easily picked that up somewhere. Read it in a book, seen it on TV. The brain's a complex organ. You've just filed the memory away somewhere and forgotten about it. But it's in there, locked away. Some stimulus has made it bubble back to the surface.'

'Okay, okay, here's a better example.' Tom's voice was becoming anxious. 'My father's father died when I was very young. I have no memory of my father's mother at all. My dad never spoke about my grandfather's family and yet I know all their names: George, Letitia, Ethelina and there were two younger sisters as well. Actually, I can't remember what they were called at the moment. But yes, there was Sarah Alice. She was the one who died. I dreamt I met them and then found them all on the 1911 census, online in the library. Their names were there in the official records, in black and white.'

Tom looked pleadingly at Jacobson, but the other man shook his head dismissively. 'Tom, it's the nature of delusions that they seem compelling and real, but you need to take a step back and listen to yourself. You're telling me that you're somehow… What? Travelling back in time? Changing places with your grandfather? Isn't that the plot of some movie or other? Listen to yourself, Tom. Is all this sensible? And this proof, the members of your grandfather's family… Isn't it much more likely that you have been told all those names, perhaps when you were very young? You've forgotten, but they're buried in your memory and it could well be the Trempatolam that's unearthing them. Here's a random thought: maybe you visited the family graveyard as a child. You either read, or someone read to you, the names on the gravestones. Now then, I suspect you don't want to believe it right now, but isn't that a far more rational explanation? Just think about it for a minute.'

Tom said nothing and the doctor took a deep breath before continuing. 'Now, this business about your grandfather doing things, as you, that you would never do. Give me an example of that.'

'He, well I, punched a colleague at work.'

'Had you been drinking?'

There was a knock on the door and Dr Jacobson raised his hand to ask Tom to hold back his answer.

'Come in, Mrs Farrell.'

The secretary craned her head around the door. 'I just wanted to remind you of the time, Dr Jacobson. Mr Haworth only has a ten minute slot.'

'Thank you, Mrs Farrell. Don't wait for us to finish; you leave at your normal time. I'll shut up shop tonight.'

'Are you sure, I just thought—'

'Please, I need to spend a little while longer with Mr Haworth and then I'll get away. Off you go now.'

The secretary flashed a resentful glance at Tom and then shut the door behind her.

The doctor turned his attention back to his patient. He spoke calmly and evenly. 'You were about to tell me if you'd been drinking when you hit your colleague.'

'The night before, yes. I guess I drank a bottle of scotch.'

'So, a man who had drunk a considerable amount of alcohol, on top of prescription medication, becomes violent. And you want to blame this on your grandfather?'

Tom wanted to continue fighting his corner, but he could see the earth slipping from the foundations of his argument. As the doctor's words sank in, the whole edifice crumbled like a sandcastle hit by a tide of reason. Tom's shoulders sank. One of the few things he took pride in was his intelligence and reason. He felt like an idiot who'd made himself look ridiculous under the light of the doctor's logic. Tom knew he should have realised it was the pills he was taking. The thought had crossed his mind, but he'd dismissed it because he'd so convinced himself that all antidepressants were ineffectual.

He smiled weakly. 'I'm sorry, doctor. I feel a total fool. I'm sure you're right.'

'Good. And don't feel bad. Drugs sometimes work very insidiously. They can cloud your reasoning without you realising. We can blame the Trempatolam. We just need to get you off it and onto something else.'

'I don't know if I want to take anything else.'

'As your psychiatrist, I would very strongly advise that you do. Just to calm you down. We'll get you back on something more established, something tried and tested. So here's the plan: go down to one Trempatolam a night for the next three days and then a day off, one pill the day after, another day off, and then one final pill. Does that make sense? That should make five in total over seven days. As I've explained before, you can experience withdrawal symptoms if you stop these treatments abruptly. Come back to see me when you're off them and we'll decide how to progress. I'll make the appointment on my computer now.'

The doctor looked at his patient carefully.

'Tom, you do accept that these dreams of yours were just that? Intense and vivid perhaps, but just dreams fuelled by the Trempatolam? And the rest of it, well, you do see it's nonsense don't you? You're not playing me along? I have convinced you, haven't I?'

Tom nodded sheepishly.

'Good. But if you have a recurrence, you phone Mrs Farrell and come in to see me urgently, you understand? And stay off alcohol for God's sake.'

'The drink isn't a problem anymore' said Tom, only dimly aware that the reason for his certainty had just evaporated away. An oath given to someone who didn't exist was as binding as a contract signed by Mickey Mouse.

Chapter twenty-three

Tom left the clinic and decided he needed some air. At the side of the grounds there was a tree-lined lane that led down to the river. If Tom then followed the towpath upstream it would take him a good part of the way home. It would add at least an hour to the journey, but he had nothing to rush back to. As he traipsed along slowly, trying to keep out of the way of commuting cyclists and early-evening joggers, he thought through what Doctor Jacobson had said and became increasingly certain of its truth. He had simply reacted badly to a drug that would soon be out of his system. Alcohol had probably been the catalyst that started the process. His dreams had been explained away convincingly. He'd never been in the trenches. His memories of Blackpool Tower Ballroom must have come from watching an episode of Strictly Come Dancing, the Big Wheel from some old documentary. Most of all, he'd never met his grandfather's family. He no longer had to worry about what happened to Clara. Someone called Clara Hargreaves was there on the 1911 census, but did that girl marry his grandfather? And if so, did she die in childbirth in 1929 or live on for another forty years? It shouldn't have been Tom's concern anymore. He wasn't personally involved, though somehow it still gnawed at him. He knew it would be healthier to forget her but he couldn't. It took him some time to recognise that, even if she was his grandfather's first wife, she wouldn't be anything like the woman in his dreams. He really had no idea of her character or what she looked like. His imaginary Clara was just a photoshopped image of his wife: Amanda with a softer smile and an attractively hooked nose. Despite this realisation, a sense of relief, of a problem gone away, still eluded him.

He got home late and went straight to bed. As normal, he struggled to get off to sleep but woke relatively early the next morning. When he opened his eyes, the first thing that entered his mind was the previous day's email to his sister and it made him wince in embarrassment. With Minnesota six hours behind, he decided to send an apology that would be waiting for her when she woke up. He couldn't face anything solid for breakfast but made himself a cup of instant coffee and sat down at his laptop. He hadn't powered it down the night before and was quickly able to check his inbox. There was one new mail item. It was from Sarah.

Dear Tommy

I've been trying to call you on your mobile but can't get through.
The kids are away on a school trip, and Jim and I were supposed to be having a few days break in San Francisco. Unfortunately, Jim's first project as department head has hit some snags and he can't afford the time away. I've traded in the flights and am coming to see you in London. I'm flying Delta via Atlanta into Terminal 4 at Heathrow and am scheduled to arrive at 8:45 am your time on Thursday, ie tomorrow. I can either stay with you or book into a hotel. If you get this in time it would be great if you could meet me at the airport, but if not I'll get the tube. Please have your damn phone with you!
Tommy, your email scared me. You don't sound at all well. Please don't do anything silly till I get there. You and I can sort this out. I promise.

Love Sarah

Tom gasped out loud, 'Oh, Sarah! No, no, no!' He scrambled for his mobile phone. It was sitting on the mantelpiece where he'd left it after his conversation with the intimidating Mrs Farrell. There were five missed calls from the same US number. He looked at his watch. It was already 7:45 am. He tried to work out if he could get to Heathrow in time. It would be touch-and-go and there was the added complication of no phone reception in the tunnels of the Underground. If he was delayed they could easily miss each other. He could call a cab, but it would likely get snarled in the rush hour traffic. He was wrestling with the problem when the mobile phone began to ring in his hand.

'Hello?'

'Hello. Tommy. It's Sarah. I'm at Heathrow. We've landed early. Tailwinds. Are you okay? You've had me so worried.'

'Sarah, I'm fine and I'm so sorry. You shouldn't have flown over. I feel so guilty.'

'Forget that. Where are you at the moment?'

'I'm at home. I only just opened your email. I was trying to work out the quickest way of getting to the airport.'

'Why don't we meet halfway. Where's the best place?'

They met at Tom's nearest tube station and took the bus back to his flat. They sat on the front seat of the top deck like they were children again, and Sarah clutched her brother's hand as tightly as she had on the journey to her first day at senior school. Tom told her he was amazed she had been able to get over so quickly and apologised repeatedly for his irrational email. He talked her through his meeting with Doctor Jacobson and tried to reassure her that everything had been explained. Sarah, in turn, said she had perhaps been a little rash, but things had slotted into place for her to make the trip, and she felt it was in some way ordained.

When they entered the flat, Tom went into the kitchen to make a cup of tea and Sarah slumped down on the sofa. She let her tiny suitcase fall on its back and shouted through to Tom, 'Do you actually live here? It's unnaturally clean and tidy.'

Tom appeared with two cups. 'It's the benefit of living on your own, but maybe I have been a bit obsessive of late. I guess I need to chill out. In more ways than one.'

Sarah smiled warmly. 'Maybe you should come back with me. Tidy our place up a bit. God knows it needs it with two messy kids and an even messier husband. Seriously though, why don't you come back with me?'

'I couldn't afford it for one thing. I dread to think how much the flights have cost you, Sis.'

'Don't worry about money. That's not important; I'm a rich American, remember? I regularly attend the Mayo Clinic, like all those ex-presidents and assorted international despots living on the wages of exploitation and corruption.'

'No, Sis, it's ridiculously generous of you, but I'm feeling so much better. It was just a bad reaction to a dodgy drug. I'll be fine.'

'Living on your own, dumped by your bitch wife, and without a job?'

'I was a drunk, Sarah. You can't blame Amanda for leaving me. And as for the job, I need to pull my finger out to find another one. Quickly. I can't go off on holiday to the States, kind as your offer is.'

Sarah hadn't been able to sleep on the way over and lay down for a couple of hours in Tom's bed. He sat quietly in his front room, and the feeling of relief that had been missing after his meeting with Doctor Jacobson finally arrived. His sister had taken on the role of protector that his father had once performed. Tom's memory of his boyhood self and his red-sweatered father at the graveyard came back, and he felt sure that, at least, was an island of truth in a sea of fantasy.

When Sarah woke in the mid afternoon, they had a late lunch. While they sat at the table, Sarah pulled out her iPhone.

'I took some photos' she said. 'I wasn't sure it would be wise to show them to you. I thought they might fuel your barminess, but as you seem to be back in the land of the sane...' She stared at Tom as if she was confirming her assessment and then continued. 'I took them quickly on the phone rather than using the scanner. They're the ones you asked for, the ones of Dad's mother. Do you want to see them, or should I delete them quickly? Would it be better to let this particular sleeping dog lie?'

Tom was almost certain the correct answer was to chloroform the dog and to tie it down with heavy weights. Unfortunately, the temptation was too great.

'No. I mean, yes, I would like to see them.'

Sarah prodded and stroked the screen and then passed the phone over. The first picture was of a woman standing with a young boy in front of a stone-built terraced house. The photograph was very dark and it was difficult to make out the faces. Both mother and son, if that's what they were, appeared to have black curly hair. The boy was slightly clearer and did look like he could be a young version of Tom and Sarah's father.

Tom flicked the image down and another took its place. Sarah noticed her brother whiten as he used his fingers to zoom in.

'Tommy, what is it? What's upset you? I knew I shouldn't have let you see them. But if you recognise anyone, it's just because you've seen the photos before. Mum or dad will have shown them to you when you were a kid. They're just buried in your memory like everything else. Like Doctor Jacobson said.'

Tom nodded slowly. 'I know, Sis. It really doesn't matter. It's all been in my mind, after all. And you're right, I must have seen this picture before. It's just that I wasn't expecting to see this face. Which is stupid of me because you'd already told me Dad got his looks from his mother. When you see them side by side, it's as clear as day.'

Tom stared at the slightly skewed image of a page from his parents' wedding album. It showed a professionally taken photograph thoughtfully labelled *The Groom's Parents*. Standing beside his mother and father were an older man and woman. The man was unmistakably Tom's namesake, his grandfather. Next to him was a handsome but buxomly overweight woman with grey hair. She had a broad smile and dimples in her cheeks. Despite the passing of the years, she was instantly recognisable. It was the woman he'd last seen, or dreamt he'd seen, at her crippled husband's funeral. It was Ann Lord.

Chapter twenty-four

Tom and Sarah stayed up past midnight whilst she extracted the full details of the delusory world that had been haunting him. She learnt of Clara, Ann, Bill, Alfred and the other players in the half-invented cast. She accepted the evidence showing that the names, if not the faces, were real. The people did exist; they had known joy, sorrow, hope and fear, but their characters in the face of such emotions could, for the most part, only be guessed at. After so much time, they would all be long dead. One or two might be distant memories in the minds of the living. The rest had become little more than paper trails: census entries and the brief three-line histories of birth, marriage and death.

Despite Tom's assurances that he recognised things for what they were, Sarah could see he still clung to a few final unravelling threads of the tightly woven cloth of his subconscious imagination. His conversation kept returning to one person, one event, one place: Clara, her death and a grave in a Pennine cemetery. He was adamant he had visited the graveyard as a young child with his father. A black marble gravestone was etched on Tom's mind, and he was tormented by gold letters he could not read. He had ordered a death certificate but it had not yet arrived, and Sarah wasn't convinced it would satisfy him and put his mind at rest. She was booked on a flight back to the States in three days time. Whilst she had been prepared to delay her return, her brother was in far better spirits than she had feared. If they could resolve the nagging issue of the gravestone, she would be able to go home to her husband and children relatively confident of Tom's mental stability. It was she, therefore, who suggested they hire a car in the morning and drive up north to the county of their birth.

Tom insisted his sister took the bed whilst he made do with the sofa. Sarah's confused body clock kept her awake, and he slept as badly as usual. As someone habituated to restless nights, he was the fresher of the two in the morning. There was a budget car hire company within a mile of the flat, and he phoned to reserve their cheapest available vehicle. Sarah made him eat something for breakfast, but they were on the road, heading for the M25, by 10:00 am.

It was a long time since she had been in a car quite so small, and the absence of an automatic gearbox saw Tom behind the wheel. The car also lacked satnav; it was of no consequence: both of them knew where they were going.

Apart from a few more motorway speed cameras and the new toll road bypassing Birmingham, the journey was little different from the years Tom had made it every few months, back when his parents were still alive. Experience told him to expect a delay due to roadworks or an accident at some point, but their progress was unhindered and they made good time. He had intended to take a break at a service station halfway, but Sarah's poor night and jet lag saw her fast asleep soon after they passed Oxford and he didn't want to disturb her. She woke as they reached Blackburn, on the final motorway leg of their route.

'Oh, Tommy, where are we? How long have I been asleep?'

'We're almost there. Just passing Blackburn. A good three hours I reckon.'

'Tommy, I'm sorry. I've been no company for you at all.'

'That's fine. You needed to sleep. You're still on Wild West time. Besides, you know I can't talk and drive at the same time. And you'd only have nagged me to slow down to 55 miles per hour' he teased.

'The federal speed limit was repealed years ago. You've been watching too many old films as usual, dearest brother. We can do 70 on the Interstates in Minnesota these days, thank you very much. I'm surprised this tiny little thing can go any faster than 55 anyway. We have real cars back home.'

'It's perfectly adequate for our purposes. I actually quite like it. I might get one if I can fool anyone into employing me again. And the film was Cannonball Run II with Daisy Duke in a Lamborghini Countach, now you mention it. She daubed a one on a speed limit sign in the desert to change it from 55 to 155 mph. Do you remember?'

Sarah sighed. 'Why would a normal person remember that?'

Tom exaggerated a puzzled expression. 'Perhaps you were never in love with Daisy Duke. Actually, she wasn't my type. The Lamborghini on the other hand... Anyway, what do you want to do? Have a quick look round Burnley first, see how much you recognise, or go straight up into the hills?'

'This isn't a nostalgia trip for me, Tommy. Let's look at that gravestone, set your mind at rest, and then maybe we can tour the sights of our supposedly regenerated hometown.'

They left the M65 at the junction before central Burnley, and the road quickly climbed into the moors leaving behind the relatively modern streets and houses which formed the outskirts of town. At one turning they passed a brown road sign labelled *Tree Panopticon*. Had Tom not been concentrating on the road he would have noticed his sister's eyebrows furrow quizzically.

'Enlighten me, Tommy.'

'Don't you have panopticon trees in the States?'

'Enlighten me, Tommy' she repeated evenly.

He relented. 'It's the Singing Ringing Tree. A tree-shaped sculpture made out of iron tubes that resonate like organ pipes when the wind blows through them. It's supposed to be quite impressive, though I've never been up close to it. You can see it from town as a distant black shape on the crest of the hills. It doesn't have any real trees to compete with, of course. It was erected a few years back and won a lot of architectural awards.'

He glanced across at his sister to see if she looked impressed and then continued, grinning. 'So, Burnley does have some tourist attractions after all. You'll be desperate to move back home at the end of this trip.'

She let out a grunt of mock indignation, and they drove in relative silence for another ten minutes until they reached the village in which their grandfather had been born and raised.

Tom's voice sounded rueful. 'Given it's so near, we hardly ever came up this way with Mum and Dad when we were young.'

Sarah looked at him across the car. 'I explained why that was. Dad's family lived round here, but his mother had fallen out with them all. She was a right bitch according to Mum, remember?'

Tom mumbled under his breath 'A beautiful bitch, though.'

'Tommy?'

'Nothing. Here we are.'

He steered the car through an open gate onto a small gravel car park, reversed back towards an old stone wall and turned off the engine.

'This is the churchyard you came to with Dad?' questioned Sarah.

Tom looked around thoughtfully. 'Yes, but there's something not right. Something's missing.'

He wasn't sure if the perceived omission came from his childhood memory or from somewhere else.

They climbed out of the car and the yellow gravel crunched underfoot. Ahead and above them was a flat-topped spur of land with a grey-black path slanting steeply up its wooded side. The trees were thicker, perhaps, but otherwise it exactly matched the image in

Tom's mind. What was missing was the church, or rather, the church was there; it just looked different and was in the wrong place.

Sarah solved the conundrum unknowingly. 'There's a plaque here. It says the car park occupies the site of the original church. It was demolished the year you were born, Tommy. Then they converted the old Sunday school into the church.'

She looked over to a large building of the far side of a few stone monuments. 'That's quite an impressive Sunday school' she said.

'It's got a new roof and been extended a bit, but no, that makes sense' said Tom distractedly.

Sarah brought him back from his reverie. 'Right. Where's this grave we've driven 250 miles to see? Up the slope you said. Does that look like what you remember from when you came here with Dad?'

'It's the same as I remember.'

Tom also recalled the deep feeling of reluctance as his eyes followed the path leading up through the trees. His sister read his unease and took him by the hand. They climbed slowly but were both slightly breathless when they reached the top. The trees parted and revealed a small grass field on which around 150 graves were arranged in a dozen rows.

Tom's expression became sombre as his eyes swept the graveyard. He had expected to be guided by a black marble stone that stood out from the others, but it was nowhere to be seen. Nonetheless, he led Sarah in an unerring direction towards the end of the second row. It was only when they got closer that he saw the stone, lying flat on its back, toppled from its plinth by decades of wind and rain.

'It's fallen over' he said unnecessarily.

The stone had inscribed gold-painted letters and was carved in the form of an opened scroll. It was partly obscured by grass which Tom ripped out in handfuls before standing back and reading the words out loud.

In Loving Memory of
CLARA,
THE BELOVED WIFE OF
THOMAS HAWORTH,
OF GARFORTH ST, BURNLEY,
WHO DIED APRIL 24th 1929,
AGED 32,
LOST WITHOUT HER

Tom felt his eyes watering. He raised his right hand to the side of his face but failed to hide the tears from his sister.

'Tommy, how are you feeling? Are you okay? It is what you expected to see, isn't it?'

'Yeh, I'm just being silly. I don't know why I'm upset. The truth is, the occupant of this grave is a complete stranger to me. If she climbed out now, I wouldn't recognise her.' He glanced at Sarah and grinned weakly. 'And not because of nearly a century's decomposition, before you mention it. I haven't the faintest idea what she looked like when she was alive.'

Sarah took his hand. 'I wonder if her photograph is anywhere in the old albums back home? You know, there are quite a few pictures with no names. It's sad. No-one's alive anymore who knows who they were.'

'There aren't any of women who bear a resemblance to Amanda are there?' asked Tom.

'If there were any that looked like your bitch wife, I'd have mentioned it, I promise.'

Tom laughed despite himself. 'Please stop calling my dear, lamented wife, the love of my life, a bitch.'

Sarah's tone became more serious. 'Was she, Tommy? Was she the love of your life?'

He said nothing in reply, but looked down at the grave in front of him and knew the answer was no.

He dropped down on his haunches, placed his right hand on the black marble gravestone and closed his eyes. When he opened them a few seconds later, Sarah questioned him gently.

'Were you saying a prayer? I didn't know you'd become religious, Tommy.'

'I haven't. It's just that I swore an oath of abstinence in those dreams and it felt really binding. Unfortunately, it was a vow given to someone who didn't really exist, so I've just repeated it to someone who did. I never knew her, but she was obviously very important to our grandfather and I'm hoping that's enough to make me keep my word. I'm getting better, getting my mind straight. The last thing I need is to hit the bottle again.'

They left Clara to her eternal rest and separated as they scanned the inscriptions on each of the other headstones across the graveyard. Some were mere initials, others told poignant stories of love, loss, tragedy and hope. The grandest monument was a six foot stone obelisk raised on a stepped base. It was dedicated to Percy Franklin Chambers, 'Much Loved Minister of this Church'. Tom stopped in its shadow and found himself wondering what sort of man Percy Chambers had really been, fire and brimstone teetotaller or placid, easygoing preacher of gentle sermons. Perhaps he was a bit of both. Tom's musings were interrupted by a shout from his sister.

'Tommy! Over here. I've found them.'

He hurried over to join her in front of a modest stone carved with three names. They read from the top chronologically: 'Precious Daughter', Sarah Alice Haworth; 'Beloved Wife and Mother', Letitia Jane Haworth; 'Much Loved Husband and Father', George Haworth.

Again, Sarah broke Tom's quiet thoughts. 'So when you came here with Dad, he must have taken you to this grave as well. You were too young to read yourself, so he'd have read out the names and told you who they were. And that's what's stuck deep in your subconscious memory.'

'No mention of Ethelina or the other sisters' observed Tom.

Sarah replied almost immediately. 'They'd get married, have their own families, fall out with Dad's mother along the way. Sorry, I don't mean to be flippant. What I'm saying is: they could be buried here under a different surname or somewhere else entirely. Or not at all, come to think of it. They were the generation for whom cremation became much more common. Grandad was cremated down in Burnley after all. Maybe Dad talked you through the whole family while you were standing here. Ethelina, in particular, is the sort of name that would stick in anyone's mind.'

'That makes sense, Sis.'

'So, Tommy, are you totally convinced? Doctor Jacobson's theory fits the facts. You do remember this place from when you came here with Dad as a child. You went straight to Clara's grave. And you could easily have picked up the other family names here as well. Or maybe Dad mentioned them some other time. Or Grandad, even. Before he died.'

Tom nodded, but said nothing as Sarah developed her case.

'And have you put this whole Clara thing to bed? You've seen the name on the black stone. You know whose grave it is. You know when she died. It's sad, I guess, but the questions have been answered. Haven't they?'

'Yes, Sis, you're right. It's all good. I'm sorted and it's all going to be fine. No more silly fantasies about people long dead.'

He had a final glance round and noticed a tall mill chimney, still standing in the middle distance as another cold stone monument to a lost past. He pointed it out to his sister and then they retraced their steps back down to the car park. They were nearly at the car when he stopped in front of one final gravestone. It, too, commemorated several members of the same family. Second from bottom, on top of mother Martha, was William Lord, who died in 1929 with 'A Life Bravely Borne'.

Tom spoke without looking at Sarah, keeping his eyes fixed on the inscription. 'I've never thought of it before. I wonder if that was why Dad was Christened William?'

She answered with a shrug and carried on walking. Halfway, she stopped and turned to look back towards her brother, who was still staring at Bill Lord's grave.

'You know, Tommy, I used to be jealous of your relationship with Dad, first born son and all that. He definitely felt a bond towards you that wasn't there with me.'

'Don't be silly, Dad loved you, Sarah. You know he did.'

'I know. And I know lots of kids have chips on their shoulders about their siblings being favourite. All the same, he was definitely closer to you. Don't take this wrongly, Tommy, but do you think you can be loved too much? You've always been the sensitive one. Do you think that's the nature you were born with or do you think Dad's affection spoilt you somehow? Spoilt's probably the wrong word, I'm sorry. But he was always so proud of you. You always worked so hard and did so well at school; you never, ever got into trouble. You couldn't do any wrong in his eyes. I'm just not sure it's the best preparation for the crap life throws at you.'

Tom looked at his sister without resentment, and it was his turn to shrug noncommittally.

They checked into a motel on a roundabout close to the motorway and spent the rest of the day exploring what remained of their childhood town. When they passed the Hop Inn, Tom was tempted to go in to test the resolve of his sobriety but knew it would be easy to be strong in the company of his sister. They ate instead in a fairly shabby Italian and shared a bottle of fizzy mineral water. First thing the next morning, they set off back to Tom's flat. They passed the afternoon and evening touring some of the sights of London - Sarah knew Manchester far better than the capital - and she caught her flight home the following day.

At the airport, Tom thanked her and apologised once more for the anxiety and expense he had caused her.

She waved the apology away. 'I've told you before, Tommy. You were the kindest big brother a girl could have and I love you very much. I'd do it again at the drop of a hat. I'm going to ask you only one thing. Email me, every day if you can. Just a few lines to tell me you're okay and to stop me worrying. Do you promise?'

'I promise, Sis.'

He watched her walk through the security gate, and once again, found himself holding back a tear.

Chapter twenty-five

Alone again, Tom busied himself with the toil of job hunting. He dug out his old curriculum vitae and set about bringing it up to date. He knew he was aggrandising his role at Mills; once he would have been nervous of being found out, but today he justified it on the basis that everyone exaggerated in their CV. He then began trawling through the plethora of job websites. He registered on several and uploaded his details. Two London-based jobs caught his eye, and he decided to apply for both.

One was in local government and required him to fill in a long questionnaire and type several pages of text explaining how he matched a list of specific requirements. His experience of EU regulations governing the bus industry came in useful when he responded to the sections on equal opportunities and health and safety. He tried to answer these in coherent English rather than glib Euro management speak, and whilst he was satisfied with the results, he wondered whether anyone would actually bother to read what he had taken so long to write.

The other job was in the private sector and it simply required him to submit his CV. All the same, he spent an hour tuning the words to emphasise those aspects of his background that seemed most relevant to the role.

It was hard work and time consuming. At the end of it all, he suspected he wouldn't even get an acknowledgement, let alone an interview. But he accepted it had to be done and the process would bear fruit eventually. A small part of him hoped Amanda might wave her magic wand again and find him a job, but he knew the last one had been a mistake and it was best that he fought this battle on his own. Besides, he and his wife had lost touch so completely now that she wouldn't even be aware he was out of work. Unless she'd discussed it in some seedy hotel room while screwing Jimmy Mills, of course.

Tom quickly put the thought out of his mind and turned on the TV. After five minutes of channel-hopping he switched it off again. In the days of his childhood three channels had provided seemingly ceaseless entertainment. There were now nearer a hundred and nothing interested him. He wondered how he could have become so much harder to please.

In the absence of distraction, he began to think of his grandfather again and what had made him marry Ann Lord. She was beautiful and available. Was he driven by simple animal lust or another desire, the need for status that Tom had sensed in his character? Did he crave the envious stares of other men? Or was he desperate for companionship after the loss of his wife? Perhaps he felt a debt towards his old friend, a responsibility to look after his supposedly grieving widow? Earlier in her life Ann would have had her pick, but what men would be available to her now? She was in her early thirties. All the one-time candidates would either be spoken for or victims of the war. Tom could see that the couple would be drawn to each other, but for his grandfather it felt like Tom's own attraction to alcohol: seductive but ultimately poisoned. Could his grandfather ever have expected Ann to replace Clara and to make him happy?

Tom stopped himself abruptly. He was once again confusing fantasy with reality. He knew nothing of his grandfather's motivations. He didn't know Ann at all. The only genuine clue to her character was provided by a single word, bitch, spoken by his mother, perhaps in a moment of anger. And when it came to her background, what did he really know? He realised he'd never seen any evidence that Ann had once been married to Bill Lord.

Tom spent the following morning checking the employment websites. There was one opening that was about to reach its deadline and which he had initially discounted because it called for an 'outgoing personality' and a 'go-getting attitude'. Even when he wore the blinkers of youthful self-confidence he wouldn't have described himself in those terms, but he applied for it anyway. If, by chance, he were to get through the initial assessment he could decide for himself if it suited him. Because of his doubts, he consciously rationed the time he devoted to completing the application.

Soon after he'd finished, he heard the letter box open and flap shut on its spring. On the doormat he found two official brown envelopes. Each contained a facsimile copy of a death certificate, outlined in black and completed by hand in 1929 and 1968 respectively. The later document was for a retired solicitor, a stranger coincidentally named Clara Haworth. The one from 1929 was for his grandfather's Clara. Having the details laid out on paper gave him a confirmation of such sombre finality that it almost surpassed the black marble headstone back in the Pennines. The informant was Thomas Haworth, husband, of Garforth Street, Burnley and present at death. The cause of death was given as Puerperal Exhaustion - the Internet revealed this to mean death due to childbirth - certified by H Morley LRCP. Tom briefly wondered if and how the baby's death would be recorded. It had escaped mention on Clara's headstone, but he decided that would be due to the sensibilities of the time. He was more concerned with the name of the doctor, H Morley, Licentiate of the Royal College of Physicians. Morley? It sounded very familiar. Was that the name he encountered in his dream? He couldn't be sure. That episode had been so painful that much of the detail had become blurred. And it was all too easy to alter memories, to confuse them with others or superimpose the present on the past in an illusion of déjà vu.

Receiving the certificates reminded Tom that there were some basic questions about his family tree that might be answered in the library. For a methodical man, he knew he had missed some obvious steps. Could he blame the Trempatolam again, or had the years of drinking addled his once reliable brain? There was information he might easily have looked for. Was his grandmother first married to Bill Lord and when did she marry his grandfather? Was she born with the name Ann Pilling? He realised he still wasn't 100% sure she was called Ann.

The library seemed to be somewhat busier on a mid week afternoon than it had been in the early morning. Fortunately, his usual computer desk was free and he sat down and logged on. He'd decided it would be better for him to work things out on his own so had simply smiled a greeting at the grey-haired librarian on the way in.

Once Tom began searching the family history website, names and dates fell quickly into line. Not for the first time, everything matched the pattern in his head with a coincidence that was convincing to the point of certainty.

He searched first for the birth entry of his father, William George Haworth. It was there, in Burnley, for the correct year and quarter. And with it, in black and white, was his mother's maiden name, Pilling. Tom searched next for a wedding between Thomas Haworth and Ann Pilling and drew a blank. He realised his mistake and looked instead for William Lord and Ann Pilling. Having found their marriage early in the First World War, Thomas Haworth and Ann Lord's union in 1930 slotted into its exact place. Tom couldn't help but feel it was all too exact. Surely distant, buried childhood memories would exhibit some gaps and inconsistencies?

Whilst searching the website's databases he stumbled on a section he had previously overlooked. It allowed other users to submit the results of their own researches, in effect their personal family trees. There was a general disclaimer suggesting these could not be relied upon, certainly not in all cases, as some contributors were less zealous than others in checking their conclusions. Whilst understanding the warning, Tom found an unmistakable link to his own family in another person's tree. Its author appeared to be descended from the Hargreaves family. Two levels back was Harold Hargreaves and his sister Clara. Clara was shown as having married Thomas Haworth before dying, childless, age 32 in 1929. Perhaps surprisingly, Thomas Haworth's lineage had also been carefully researched along with all the Hargreaves.

The tree extended both up and down the generations, with question marks in a few places where the researcher had drawn a blank. The surviving members were given anonymity by being recorded as 'Living Hargreaves', as well as 'Living Evans' and 'Living Lewandowska', intermarriage having brought surnames from beyond East Lancashire into the more recent family.

Tom was unable to ascertain which of the living members might be the author of the tree. The contact email address, JaneJust@..., didn't seem to relate to any of the names and surnames he could see. As Tom pondered what, if anything, he might learn from this unexpected source, a message flashed up warning him that his allotted time on the library computer would expire in three minutes. He was only able to send a rushed message to JaneJust before he was logged off.

He returned home contemplating how much he should reveal to Sarah in his next email. He decided to report the names and dates that he had found, but downplay any concerns he might have about the precision with which they matched his memories. After all, he told himself, there was still Trempatolam in his system. It might yet be playing tricks with his mind and clouding his judgement. The last thing he wanted to do was cause her more anxiety.

Chapter twenty-six

Jane Evans slumped down on the thin grass next to the stone marker that signified her climb was over. Her fleece was knotted round her waist by its arms. It had been relegated from vital warmth to irksome burden when the early morning clouds had drifted away over the Channel towards France. Now the exertion of reaching the top conspired with the midday heat to make her feel almost overdressed in t-shirt and shorts.

The plateaued summit of the sea cliff was green with grass and bracken, but the yellow sandstone outcrop beneath had glowed in the sunlight like the gold of an archer's target as Jane zigzagged towards it up the steep coastal path. She had wanted to walk the Dorset coastline and climb Golden Cap, the south coast's highest point, for a decade or more. Her husband had always overruled and insisted on foreign beach holidays with their guarantee of good weather. His job had been stressful, and she'd felt it was only right to surrender to his will and to give him the break he'd desperately deserved.

Jane stood up and looked down the gently curving arc of Lyme Bay with its ivory sands washed by a manganese blue sea. She wished she had her paints with her and had to make do with a photograph taken on her mobile phone. Tony had planned on early retirement in 10 or so years' time. She thought of the freedom it would have given them. Perhaps she could have convinced him to walk the whole 630 miles of footpath that ran round the cliffs, bays and estuaries of England's south west corner. They could have stayed in pretty little seaside towns along the way, absorbed the light and painted together, like they used to when they were at art school.

His heart attack had put an end to any dreams of comfortable retirement. She'd been left with a huge, unpayable mortgage on their Manchester home and twin sons away at university, running up debts they would now have to pay off on their own. Losing their father had been hard for the boys, and it had been particularly difficult for them to accept the embarrassment of his being struck down in his secretary's bed whilst supposedly away on a business trip. Jane had felt hurt and betrayed as any wife would, though she knew his punishment had exceeded his crime. He was a man who'd always expected forgiveness whatever his misdemeanour, and she found herself wondering, once again, if she'd always been played for a fool. Then she felt the sunshine on her face and took in the magnificence of the view. It was a sight he would now never enjoy. She knew she should count her blessings. She had never been the greatest of beauties, but time had been relatively kind to her figure and face. Her health was good, though she appreciated more than ever that it could not be taken for granted. Tony had played squash as aggressively as when he was a young man, and despite his spreading waistline, would have boasted of his strength and vigour.

Moving away from her friends had been a wrench, but back in her hometown of Blackburn, property prices were much more affordable. It had also meant she could spend time with her mother, whose own health had started to deteriorate rapidly. Together they had worked on expanding the family tree that the older woman had first fleshed out in the days before the Internet. When she'd been more mobile, she'd enjoyed day trips to London visiting the old Family Records Centre, but progress working through the huge books of printed indexes - with red covers for births, green for marriages and black for deaths - had been slow. With the aid of the Web, mother and daughter had been able to share a hobby and fill in many of the gaps with relative speed. They'd proudly loaded the results of their efforts onto the website when it became clear the older woman's end was close. Then, in her final hours, she'd revealed to her daughter a family secret that would otherwise have been lost forever. Like a tree falling in a forest, unheard and philosophically noiseless, it would never have happened. Jane had always known her mother abhorred deception but had been saddened to learn she'd endured decades worrying about unlikely official retribution for a victimless crime of which she, for certain, was totally innocent. The family tree was both an insight into who she was and a gentle act of defiance from a woman who could no longer be punished.

Chapter twenty-seven

Tom put his laptop back on his knee and began idly searching the Internet. He checked the news from the BBC and then the sport. He was by no means a football fan but tried to follow Burnley's results on at least an intermittent basis. When he found them, he wished he hadn't and pressed the home button to take him back to a blank search page.

For some reason he typed *Trempatolam*.

As with nearly every Google search there were half a million results, but high on the list were some recent news articles discussing the controversy over the drug in America. One of them led him to a website newly set up by a help group for 'victims' of Trempatolam. As Tom read through its stated aims, it was fairly obvious that the primary goal was to get people together in readiness for suing the drug company for all it was worth. But there were also forum pages where people could discuss and share their reactions to Trempatolam, and in doing so, learn from the experience of others and hopefully ease their anxieties. After a slow start, contributions were now being added at a rate of three or four a day.

Some of forum messages were laced with hyperbole and ungrammatical ranting, and Tom thought it was obvious why their authors needed medication. Then he remembered his own unbalanced email to his sister and reprimanded himself for being judgmental.

In amongst emotional tales of blighted lives and suicidal thoughts, and complaints about unhelpful doctors and profit-obsessed drug companies, Tom began to see a recurring theme. It wasn't in all cases, certainly, but in a number too significant to be random. At first it gave

Tom reassurance that his own experiences could be blamed away on Trempatolam, but then it started raising fresh questions in his mind. The pattern he saw was being consistently discounted by the psychiatric profession, and Tom would normally have dismissed it out of hand himself. In the language of his childhood, he would have called it 'plain barmy', though he was sure the doctors would have used kinder, or perhaps better disguised, terminology. Because of his own experience, however, he read and re-read certain stories and became increasingly convinced that something unusual was happening.

Hallucinations, intense dreams and nightmares were commonly reported side effects of the drug. Some people described hearing voices or seeing strange apparitions, but several talked of visions of past lives. One of the latest submissions was from a man who recalled labouring as an Egyptian slave building the Great Pyramid. Another contributor told of being Custer himself at the Battle of the Little Bighorn. But some of the earlier postings featured less grandiose stories. It was to these more prosaic reports that Tom kept returning. Four in particular were spelt out in illuminating detail.

Maddie75

I need to share my own experiences with Trempatolam. They've been hard to put into words and I warn you, you're going to be shocked. Please don't judge me. Please remember I was affected by this evil drug that's poisoned all of us.

Just for background - I live in Little Rock, AR. I'm in a good, long-term relationship with another woman and we run an online business together. I've had a few problems in the past and about a year back found myself in a really dark place. My partner made me get help and I was prescribed Trempatolam. After a few weeks I started having these crazy, crazy dreams that were just so real. In one, I was looking through my mother's eyes on the day of her wedding to my father. I've never been married, but I felt the tingling excitement and anticipation of a young bride. I saw myself in a flowing white dress. I sat in the shiny Cadillac driving me to church. He's been in a wheelchair for years, but my grandpa walked me down the aisle. When I reached the altar, there was my father like I'd never seen him before - skinny, dark haired and so, so handsome in his elegant tux. Everything was in such clear, intricate detail. And then later, I saw the wedding night. I was myself, but somehow inside my mother's head. I felt a combination of joy, desire, pain and disgust, filthy disgust, as I experienced my own father, insatiable and rough, doing what men do on wedding nights. I feel sick and I'm crying as I write this.

In a later episode, I felt the heartbreak of discovering my husband/father's first infidelity and I watched my hand shake as I gripped the razor that sliced into my wrist. I can see myself now - I'm cutting and cutting, but I just can't find the vein.

I told all this to my clinician and he said it was a classic example of a Jungian 'Electra Complex'. He suggested that the guilt from my suppressed childhood desires for the father who walked out on us when I was ten could have contributed to the development of my own sexuality. Maybe that's true, but the thing is, I never knew about my mother's suicide attempt. I asked her and she's confessed to me now, but I didn't know before. It happened a year before I was born and my conception was a failed attempt at rebuilding the marriage. Again I told the doctor, but he said there would have been scars on my mother's wrist and that I must have recognised them for what they were but denied the unpalatable truth.

I guess he's right, but it all seemed so real. Trempatolam has so much to answer for. I don't think they should get away with ruining people's lives like this. If it wasn't for my partner's support I might have followed my mother's example. But we keep a LadySmith .38 Special and I'd have done the job properly.

MethodMan

hi. im a codemonkey for a startup in silicon valley. im geek to the core and proud of it. give me any test and ill give you a pretty high score on the autism spectrum. being high functioning aspergers is kinda cool round here but i found i was getting more and more withdrawn hiding from people and never going out. they put me on tremps and at first it was great. all day at the keyboard writing sweet zero bug java code and every night down the bar with the guys. well not every night tbh but pretty often anyways. and then i started getting the weird dreams. im the most non confrontational guy you could ever meet but my dad owns a construction company and is as mean as you like to everyone but me. he grew up on the wrong side of the tracks and never speaks about his own father except to say he was a total and utter b*****d that you wouldnt want to mess with. in these dreams im my own grandfather but as a young guy stealing and getting into fights. one time i get beat up bad by a cop. the cops hitting me with his billystick over and over again until im nearly dead. s**t it hurt. in the next dream im waiting in a backalley. its night and im really scared and tense. the same cop walks by. i freeze but he sees me and comes right at me. blam blam blam. im so scared and i shoot at him with the gun ive got. i can hear the shots now. blam blam blam. im so scared i think i miss but the cop dives for cover and i run off down the alley. i just keep running and running. i can hear the sirens screaming now. ive never had dreams like this. its like i was just there. like im remembering it from my own life. i dont want to look like a psycho in front of my doc so i havent told him. i certainly havent told my dad because he doesnt know ive been on medication. he already thinks im a total pussy. he was actually pleased when i told him i got punched in a bar a few weeks back. it was so unlike me to get into a fight. it was something to do with a girl but i really cant remember it properly. i guess i was totally wasted. im betting it was down to the Trempatolam again. hey thats my story. how much do you guys think the drug company will have to pay out for the s**t theyve caused.

KatharineK

I've been intrigued by the accounts of other contributors describing realistic dreams that set them back in the lives of their antecedents. They closely mirror my own experiences with Trempatolam, though I find it difficult to understand why we should be sharing such an effect.

My father was an attorney and senior partner in a successful Boston law firm but achieved his success despite a relatively impecunious upbringing. His mother's first husband was bankrupted at the onset of the Great Depression with ultimately tragic consequences.

I, myself, have enjoyed a privileged life but have been plagued by the same mental frailty that afflicted my long-suffering mother in later life. At various times, I have been under medication but have never been wholly satisfied by the efficacy of the drugs prescribed. The benefits attributed to Trempatolam were appealing, and I persuaded my psychiatrist that I should be one of its first recipients.

When I started on the course of treatment, I did notice an initial improvement but this may have been illusory. One never knows whether one is a dupe to that optimism of new hope otherwise known as the placebo effect.

I was advised to avoid alcohol if at all possible, and apart from the occasional social function, was able to comply. It may be coincidental, but after one particular lapse in this regard, I had the first in a succession of disturbing dreams. I use the word but feel 'dream' is an inadequate description of the episodes I experienced. I would wake having almost totally forgotten the previous day of my true existence - perhaps because of its largely routine banality - but find it overlaid in my mind by a much more intense and fresh recollection of almost uncanny realism: a memory of a day seemingly from another's life, that person being my father's own mother, a lady who passed on some sixty years ago when I myself was in my teens.

I will not describe the content of my dreams in any great detail. They are personal and, as such, only of interest to the voyeur. Suffice to say, I experienced what must have been the points of zenith and nadir in her early life. At first it was wonderful. I saw the roaring twenties, extravagant parties and a young woman of great beauty pursued by handsome, wealthy men, all vying for her hand in marriage. If I close my eyes, I can feel now the joy, gaiety and excitement of it all. I almost burn with jealousy not to have lived such a life myself. The suitors led to courtship and then the most extravagant of weddings. Bride and groom moved into a fine townhouse on the

Upper East Side, Manhattan. I saw the passage of time summarised in specific events, sometimes days, sometimes months apart.

I began living my own life impatiently waiting for night to fall, in the hope that I might be transported back to this magical world. But then the dreams changed abruptly. The day her husband did not come home, the day the stock market crashed, the policeman at the door, the shocking news of a bankrupted man taking his own life, the threat of destitution. From unscalable high to pitiful low we, she and I, sank. I lived her desperation as she gave herself to a man far beneath her in manners and breeding. I suppose you could say he had a good, stable job but he wasn't able to keep her in the style to which she was accustomed. She accepted a humble lifestyle for a roof over her head. I know they were trying times, but I would have made her wait. Someone of such beauty could have held out for someone so much better. She should have left him; however, she was soon pregnant with my father's elder brother, and it became too late.

There you have it. I have told you more than I intended; make of it what you will. With my father dead, I cannot confirm the fine detail of any of my dreams, although they fit what scant facts are available to me. From my personal perspective, whilst Trempatolam ultimately left me dispirited and desolate, it feels, perhaps, a worthwhile trade for the earlier happiness and escape it gave to me.

Mackdriver

I'm a truck driver. Big 240 pound guy. The sort of guy who ain't supposed to get depression. I live in Pittsburgh now but I grew up in hicksville USA. My folks had a genuine mom and pop grocery store. My dad was always quiet. Mom dealt with all the suppliers and most of the folks in the store. Dads main thing seemed to be doing the books and keeping the shelves tidy. Looking back now and knowing what I know the guy was suffering from depression himself but that's not something you understand as a child. I'm not even sure they called it depression back then. When they put me on trempatalam I felt good at first but then I started getting the dreams too. In these dreams my dad is a really clever kid and they think he might go to college to be lawyer or a doctor. His father works 2 jobs trying to get the money together. My dad is studying so hard and really trying to make his parents proud. In the end he falls apart. Can't handle it no more. Takes to his bed and lays there crying. His father just don't understand how someone who has the chance to make something of himself can throw it away. He gets really mad. Thats what I dreamt anyway. No big drama I guess in the scheme of things but it made me feel really low. The doc says its not unusual to dream about our parents and I should use it as a positive in understanding my relationship with my father. There's one strange thing that bugs me though. In my dream of the day my dad finally fell apart he was studying one particular thing. He kept reading it over and over again trying to understand it. It wouldn't seem to go in and he was getting more and more upset. It was one of those chemical formulas. I was a total dumbass at school and I haven't a clue but I was able to write it out for the doc and he said it was called something like a stockymetric equation and it looked right. The doc said I must have picked it up somewhere but he looked at me kinda suspicious as if I was playing some kinda game. Anyway I'm just glad I'm not taking trempatalam no more. Its enough trying to deal with my own problems without having my head filled with my dads too. Even if I am just imagining them.

Tom sat back on his sofa and tried to organise his thoughts. There was a clear common thread running through each of these stories. There were three or four others which were less detailed, but reading between the lines, appeared similar in pattern. People had found themselves in the shoes of a direct ancestor, one or two generations removed. They had seen vivid snapshots of their parent's or grandparent's life, nearly always at times of great pain or great joy, the sort of events that no-one ever forgets, that they can close their eyes and return to until the final spark of life is extinguished.

Tom could see that Mackdriver's doctor was right: we do dream about our parents. But there was an intensity of experience that the doctor couldn't understand, or perhaps, wasn't willing to accept. Then there was Mackdriver's chemical formula and the attempted suicide of Maddie75's mother. Suggestions of insight that could be explained away but still made Tom question. Why would people from different parts of America, with varied backgrounds, share very similar experiences to his own? Surely drug induced dreams would be totally random and inconsistent? What part of the brain could Trempatolam be stimulating to cause such a reaction?

After some consideration, Tom added his own story to the website but left the details vague and unattributable. He feared his sister might stumble on the forum and recognise his contribution. He didn't want to expose his returning doubts and cause her any more anxiety than he already had.

Chapter twenty-eight

Tom had weaned himself off Trempatolam as the doctor had instructed and had taken his final pill. That night he experienced one final, brief dream of his grandfather, dancing this time with Ann Pilling. They began on the dance floor but spun and swirled up amongst the figures painted in the clouds on the ballroom's ceiling. Sarah appeared, tapped Tom on the shoulder and pulled him back down to earth.

When Tom awoke it was a shadowy memory, but he recognised it as a normal and explicable meandering of his subconscious. Even so, it prompted him to turn on his laptop and visit the Trempatolam victims' forum yet again. There were two new entries of note. One was from a woman in Rhode Island who said she'd seen herself as Joan of Arc burning at the stake, but the other was from a 35 year-old African American who described experiencing degrading incidents of racial prejudice suffered by his father in 1960s Alabama.

An idea had been forming in Tom's head. He heard his sister and Doctor Jacobson telling him to ignore it, but it wouldn't go away. He neglected his job hunting and spent the next two days trawling the Internet looking for evidence to prove or disprove his hypothesis. It wasn't long before he was immersed in documents of complex technicality, using language and terms barely intelligible to someone whose scientific knowledge was limited to distant, half-remembered schooldays.

He needed help. He knew one person who could provide it, and it would be Dangerous.

The pun made him smile. Dangerous Dave Dunstan, the man he had been avoiding for six months or more because of the threat he posed. The brightest person Tom knew, arguably the funniest and also one of the most easily distracted. The one who had become obsessed with amateur dramatics at university and failed his degree as a result. But the degree he failed was in Molecular Biology and he had gone on to work in medical research. If anyone could decipher this stuff, it was Dave.

They'd lived in the same student hall of residence. It was Tom's fresher year, and he came down to breakfast on the first morning feeling somewhat lost and overawed by being away from home for the first time. He'd opted for a fully catered hall and loaded up his tray with an overambitious amount of food before looking round the canteen for a friendly face. His natural inclination was to sit on his own, but it was a new chapter in his life and he was making a conscious effort to be brave. The faces he saw seemed to be a mixture of the uncomfortable - presumably first years like himself - and the confident. The latter were chatting away to the other people on their table like they were old friends. Some of them would be returning students catching up with their mates after the long summer break, but Tom knew that many would be the type of self-assured person who just found such things easy. It was a male-only establishment, so Tom didn't have the complication of trying to weigh girls' attractiveness against his own. His eyes scanned across the heads and stopped at one that stood out. It was higher than most of the others and was crowned by an Afro of reddish-blond curls. Its owner sat at a table on his own; he was smiling away to himself, and Tom decided he looked approachable. Tom had long ago pigeonholed himself as a Second Division personality. At school he didn't try to mix with the really cool kids - the First Division whom everyone liked and always seemed to be in the school team, whatever the sport - yet he usually avoided the real geeks and nerds who formed the lower leagues. Blond Afro looked somewhat geekish, but Tom decided it was safer to aim low.

'Is it okay if I sit here?' he asked.

'No worries, Bruce' said Blond Afro, who then stood up to shake Tom's hand before introducing himself.

'My name's Dave, Dave Dunstan.'

Tom was reasonably tall and wasn't used to looking up at people, but Dave seemed to tower over him and the mop of hair exaggerated the effect. His shoulders, however, were very narrow and his oversize clothes hung loosely over a wiry frame. He had metal-rimmed aviator glasses and a tightly curled ginger beard that only grew beneath his jaw. His accent was indeterminate. All Tom knew was that it wasn't northern.

'I'm Tom, Tom Haworth. Are you Australian?'

'Nah, sorry about that. I'm from Guildford. It's a bit of a joke among my friends back home. We all talk in Australian accents and call each other Bruce. It's Monty Python's fault. I'm sure you remember the Bruce sketch? I guess I'm stuck in the habit. Where are you from? Is it your first year?'

Tom's own school friends could recite most of the Python canon, which had always seemed far funnier in repetition. He nodded and answered Dave's other questions. 'I'm down from Burnley, you know, Lancashire. And yes, it's my first year. I'm sure you can tell; how about you?'

'Yes and no. I was studying Chemistry last year but I had a friend doing Molecular Biology and it seemed much more interesting. DNA and all that. I've switched courses and started again. I wasn't in halls last year; I was commuting from Guildford which was a real drag. Made me feel right crook, Bruce, as we say back home.'

Tom and Dave, or Dangerous Dave as he was known in the Surrey Outback for reasons of alliteration only, became good friends. They were both studious, in that first year at least, and they shared a hobby: they both liked

159

a drink. Each of them was studying a subject where the men outnumbered the women; neither was blessed with a great deal of confidence where the opposite sex was concerned, and they lived in all-male accommodation. As a result, their social life revolved around cheap student bars and drinking with the boys. Both were proud of their capacity to down copious amounts of alcohol and still make it to lectures the following day. By the third year their paths began to diverge. Dave discovered the Dramatic Society and Tom found Christine, his first real girlfriend, who was tall and thin with mid brown hair and hazel eyes. The two men did, however, keep in touch when they left university. They both stayed in London and met up every few weeks for a session in one bar or another. Despite failing his degree, Dave worked in the pharmaceutical industry for a while and stumbled on a talent for technical writing. Eventually, he went freelance. He earned just enough to fund his drinking, and self-employment meant he could accommodate his declining powers of recovery and sleep off his daily hangovers. He would type at his computer late into the night with a glass of scotch ever-present alongside his mouse. He would swear a 'cheeky snifter' helped the words flow and made him a better writer. He never married, and despite his regular exhortations to 'Look at the koala bears on that sheila, Bruce!' Tom began to wonder if he was gay. His long on-off relationship with the frightening Betty had always seemed more fraternal than physical. In their university days, coming out of the closet was a brave decision, but the world had changed since then and it seemed strange for an old friend not to open up. If Dave was living in denial, it would be about more things than one. He was adamant he didn't have a problem with alcohol. He was a social drinker who drank on his own only because it made his work better. That was what made him dangerous to be with as far as Tom was concerned and why they hadn't seen each other for so many months.

The phone was answered after the third ring.

'G'day.'

'Is that Dave Dunstan, also known as Dangerous Dave Dunstan?'

'Bruce! How are you, cobber? It's been so long! I seem to recall you were avoiding me because I was such a wicked influence. Don't tell me, that sexy, intelligent wife of yours has seen sense and stopped nagging you about your slight fondness for the golden nectar, so you've phoned up to ask your old mate out for a tube or two. Like the bonzer days of old, eh?'

'Ah, Dave, I've missed you. And yes, Amanda has stopped nagging me. She nags someone else these days. My slight fondness, as you put it, was too much for her in the end. I'm sorry I haven't been in touch. I couldn't afford for you to lead me astray. Again. They were good old days, you're right, but you can't go back. I can't go back. I'm a very boring, sober person now. A very boring, sober person who is battling with a scientific conundrum and needs to pick the brains of nearest person he knows to Albert Einstein.'

There was a slight delay before a reply came back from the other end of the line. 'Two things, Bruce. One: I'm sorry to hear about Amanda. She always hated my guts - to be fair, she was always a good judge of character - and she was never over-endowed in the koala bear department, but I know how much she meant to you. Two: Einstein? That sounds like flattery to me. Since when did you become a smooth-talking bastard, or as we say back home, a smooth-talking pommy bastard?'

'Sorry, Dave. It's just that something is really bugging me at the moment and I need some help. You are the nearest person I know to the great, wild-haired, moustachioed one, and to tell you the truth, you're the only mate I've got left - assuming you're still talking to me after all this time. Even if you didn't know your nucleotide sequence from your extended phenotype, I'd still appreciate the opportunity of talking this through with you. It's pretty mad, if I'm honest.'

'Pretty mad? Then you're talking to the right man, bossfella. Which of our old watering holes, or to use the correct Australian term, billabongs, shall we meet up in?'

'I've never been convinced that is the correct Australian term, Dave, and here's the thing: I was thinking more of a mid morning cappuccino rather than a lunchtime or evening session in a boozer. I really, really don't do those anymore.'

'Mid morning? Cappuccino? CAPPUCCINO? Strewth, cobber! Good job you're my oldest mate. I'll do you a deal; late morning cappuccino and I'll be there.'

They met the next day in a West End coffee shop belonging to one of the big chains that seemed to have swamped central London. Dave pretended to be dazzled by the exotic selection of coffees and let Tom order. They sat facing each other at a small table in the window, and Dave winced as he brought the foamy cup to his lips.

'Stop pulling faces' said Tom. 'It's good for you. Well, it's not particularly, but it's better than booze.'

'Tastes like dingo piss to me, cobber. Hot, frothy dingo piss.'

'How would you know what dingo piss, hot or otherwise, tastes like? I know they drink little else Down Under, but unless there's something I don't know, you've never been anywhere near Australia. Cobber.' Tom pronounced it *Orst*ralia in an exaggerated accent.

'That's because I'm not convinced they'd appreciate my sense of humour. On the other hand, I might blend right in. You know, given that I speak the lingo, they'd probably take me for a native, one of their own.' Dave's face was deadpan serious.

Tom mirrored his friend's expression. 'Almost certainly.'

'But then, of course, the other problem with me getting into Australia is my criminal record.'

Tom looked at Dave quizzically before he remembered the old joke. 'The fact you don't have one?' he sighed.

Dave grinned and raised his eyebrows in confirmation before spotting a moderately buxom young woman walking past the window.

'Cor Murrumbidgee! Look at the koalas on that sheila!' he exclaimed.

'Murrumbidgee? That's a new one on me' puzzled Tom.

'Ah, there's a story there' grimaced Dave. You may remember that my exclamation of choice used to be: Cor Wagga Wagga! Now, you and I know Wagga Wagga is the name of a genuine, bona fido Australian town. It's not my fault that the first 'a' is pronounced more like an 'o'. Unfortunately, I was in a bar recently and some blokes thought I was being racist and got a bit shirty with me. Well, one of them thumped me actually—'

'I always told you it was a stupid thing to say' interrupted Tom.

'Well, okay, you were obviously right. I didn't mean to cause anyone any offence, but clearly I did. So now it's: Cor Murrumbidgee! The mighty Murrumbidgee being the river on which the metropolis that is Wagga Wagga sits. The Tiber to the Outback's Rome, the Seine to the Paris of New South Wales. Etcetera.' Dave beamed with satisfaction.

Tom shook his head. 'And while we're at it, commenting on women's koalas isn't exactly acceptable these days. If it ever was.'

Dave smirked like a naughty child. 'I only said that for your benefit. I know it's one of your favourites, even if you pretend it's not.'

Tom laughed reluctantly and then pointed at the other man's neck. 'And since when have you started wearing ties?'

'It's called style, you wouldn't understand. And my dad used to swear by these ties.'

Dave's face was deadpan again and the punch line was timed to perfection.

'"Fucking ties" he used to say.'

They chatted for a while to catch up on recent events. Dave's life had altered little, though it seemed to have aged him noticeably since Tom last saw him. The red-blond curls ringing his bald pate had faded and his whole face appeared greyer and more sallow. Tom enquired after his friend's health, but the question was waved away dismissively. Inevitably, the conversation soon focussed on Tom's own more dramatic story, and he talked at some length to bring his friend up to date.

'So this forum has several people reporting past life experiences?' clarified Dave.

'Exactly.'

'Most likely explanation is copycat behaviour, of course. Nutters...' Dave raised an apologetic hand. 'Sorry, I'm not saying you're a nutter, Bruce. Well, not a fully fledged one anyway. But as I was saying, *nutters* traditionally fancy themselves as God or Napoleon or Cleopatra, don't they? And then there's mass hysteria. I'm sure you've heard about Orson Welles' radio production of *The War of the Worlds* in America in the 1930s. It was presented as if it were a live news broadcast. People who tuned in halfway through thought they were hearing real reports of a Martian invasion. Then loads of them convinced themselves they'd seen aliens too, and the police were inundated with calls. Actually, they now reckon it was a myth created by the press at the time, but it makes you think. It's not quite the same as what you're talking about, I suppose, but it still makes you think. Or maybe not.'

Tom looked disappointed. 'Did I compare you to Einstein? Look, I understand some of the stories could be copycat fantasies, and I've certainly got my doubts about Custer and Joan of Arc, but I, for one, am not copying anybody. What I really wanted to pick your brains about is epigenetics. What do you know about epigenetics?'

'Epigenetics! What don't I know about epigenetics?' exclaimed Dave, closely followed by 'Epi..? What was the word again?' His face then became serious and thoughtful. After a few seconds he nodded. 'I see where you're going. There's a lot of controversy surrounding the field of epigenetics at the moment - and you're way out on the boundaries of what it might explain - but I see where you're going. There's one key question, I guess. Ignoring Alexander the Great and Pocahontas, just focussing on those people going back one or two generations of their own direct ancestors, did all the memories predate their own birth or, in the two generation cases, that of their parent?'

Tom's expression turned to one of hope. 'As far as I can tell, yes. Predated their conception, in fact' he said.

Tom arrived early as usual for his appointment at the clinic. This time he went straight to the windowless waiting room. Mrs Farrell was in her lair and she greeted him with an unconvincing smile. The phrase 'Come into my parlour...' flashed into his mind before she interrupted his thoughts.

'Ah, Mr...' She made a conscious display of looking at her computer screen, '...Haworth, thank you for arriving promptly. Will you be paying by card today? It will save us some time if we get the process out of the way now. Would you mind?'

It was clearly an instruction rather than a request, and her previous assessment of Tom's character made her unprepared for the equally unequivocal response.

'Actually, let's leave it until afterwards. I have to get my thoughts together for Dr Jacobson. I'm sure you understand, Mrs Farrell. Thank you.'

Her head twisted in an acknowledgment that was neither nod nor shake, and she turned silently back to her computer. The trivial victory gave Tom a brief moment of satisfaction that faded when he imagined himself in her shoes, dealing with difficult and unbalanced patients on a daily basis. He tried to catch her eye to offer a conciliatory grin, but she remained fixed on her screen.

He had always assumed that his free allowance of the psychiatrist's time would have come to an end. Despite his limited finances, he was glad. He was paying for a service and would feel no guilt about how he used it.

The soundproofed door opened, and a young man with reddened eyes left Dr Jacobson's office in some haste. After a short delay, the doctor himself appeared at the door. He looked as if he'd had a tiringly long day.

'Tom, would you come in please?'

Tom sat in the upright armchair facing the desk, and Dr Jacobson took his place behind it.

'So, Tom, how have you been? You're looking well.'

'Thank you. I feel good. My sister came over from America for a few days. We went up to our home town in Lancashire and talked a few things over. It really helped get some things clear in my mind.'

'Excellent! That sounds really positive. It's a shame your sister doesn't live closer. We all need someone to talk to, someone we trust. But I guess, with the Internet these days, it's easier to keep in touch whatever the distance. Keep talking to your sister, Tom. That's probably the best advice I can give you.'

Tom looked at the other man, who was partially silhouetted by the brightening sky in the window behind him. The setting reminded Tom of a job interview. He knew that he would once have treated it as such: he would have tried to please, to give the doctor the answers he wanted to hear. That was not going to happen today. It was a different Tom who took control of the conversation.

'There's something I haven't told my sister. Not yet, anyway. I don't want to cause her any more worry than I have already. I've talked it over with a friend who's got a certain level of expertise, and I wanted to use you as a sounding board, too.'

Dr Jacobson's eyebrows dropped perceptibly.

'What are your friend's qualifications, precisely?'

'Well, he never actually passed his degree, but he knows his stuff.'

'Go on' said the doctor.

'Okay, there's a Trempatolam forum on the Internet. People are writing about their experiences.'

'Yes. One of my colleagues drew my attention to it a few days ago.'

'Good, I'm glad you've read it.'

Jacobson's eyebrows sank lower. Despite his efforts at disguise, his expression now spoke of concern, or perhaps irritation.

'I'm a busy man. Outside of patients, I have a lot of paperwork, plus formal research journals and the like to keep on top of. I glanced through the forum. I think I read enough to get the general idea.'

'But did you see a pattern? Did it remind you of my experiences?' prodded Tom.

The doctor answered wearily. 'Trempatolam has been widely prescribed in the States, far more so than over here. I saw a tiny percentage of recipients describing symptoms of, what shall we call it, past life regression? They ranged from building the pyramids to sleeping with their father. I saw a steady increase in reports after a slow start. What did you see, Tom?'

'In amongst the pyramids and Joan of Arc, I saw several people with very similar experiences to my own. They lived through episodes of one of their parent's or grandparent's lives. Sometimes they discovered information they couldn't otherwise have known.'

'Tom, please, we've been through this. Trempatolam may be unlocking a few long-forgotten childhood memories. But then you're building a whole delusionary world on top of them.'

'But wouldn't delusions be more random? This seems to be a very specific effect. Would a drug do that? I mean, do the same thing to multiple people?'

'Tom, you're an intelligent man. I suspect you've heard of collective obsessional behaviour. This seems very similar. One person reports something, someone else hears about it or reads about it, and particularly if they're emotionally vulnerable, they convince themselves the same thing's happened to them. Before long you have an outbreak of cases. You know, some studies suggest that four million Americans would claim to have been abducted by aliens. Oh, for goodness sake! People can talk themselves into believing anything. If they find it appealing in some way, they can convince themselves it happened to them. Also, let's not forget the possibility of some individuals wanting to exaggerate their symptoms in the hope of getting compensation. Be honest with me, Tom; do you have any expectations in that respect?'

Tom ignored the doctor's direct question and asked one of his own. 'Are you saying I went on the Internet, read the forum and then made up my story?'

'I'm saying you've been under the influence of a drug with known delusional effects, and whilst you probably believe what you're telling me, we - that's both of us - should treat it with some scepticism. You were talking about time travel, remember?'

'I'm not sure I was ever talking about time travel. Well, maybe I was leaning that way once. It did seem for a while like I was swapping places with my grandfather, like he was doing things in my place. Now I accept that the Trempatolam, combined with alcohol, was affecting my behaviour. And maybe some of my experiences over the last few weeks have changed me, perhaps for the better. There were incidents that seemed strangely distant, as if I wasn't there, but I can only assume they were drowned out by the intensity and realism of the dreams I was having. Doctor, those dreams... My theory is that I'm unlocking what are called transgenerational memories. Things burnt indelibly into my grandfather's mind that have been passed down to my father and then to me. Things buried so deeply that they're only unearthed in exceptional circumstances, like when you're under the influence of a particular drug.'

The doctor shook his head. 'Forgive me. I don't want to belittle your ideas, but that sounds like pseudoscientific mumbo jumbo. People have been using hypnosis, for example, to unearth so-called past lives since at least the 1950s. They dig up ancestors or, if you believe in reincarnation, they can find memories of anyone you fancy. You too can be the Duke of Wellington at Waterloo. I'm sorry, Tom, I don't mean to be facetious, but the scientific community regards this stuff with the utmost scepticism. You need to stop clinging to it. I'm not mincing my words, because I think you're stable and intelligent enough to see the truth.'

Tom responded with a question. 'Do you think memories can be inherited?

'No' came the blunt response.

Tom continued. 'Birds are born with an innate ability to build nests. It's accepted they don't learn from their parents. Birds from artificially incubated eggs, raised in isolation, still build nests. Different species build different types. Some, like weaver birds, use complex construction techniques. It's the same as spiders spinning intricate webs. What's that if not an inherited memory? In some form or another, they must have a picture in their mind of what they're aiming towards and the steps required to get there. Do you agree?'

'I don't accept that's a memory; it's an inherited behaviour or instinct. And as you said, different species build their own types of nest. That's the nature of inheritance. We get our DNA from our parents, 50% from each, and it's throughout our cells at birth. The important point is: it's fixed and immutable. If our parents are born with the ability to build a certain type of nest, we build the same nest. We can't learn how to build a better one and magically reprogram our DNA so that our offspring know instinctively how to build it too. They're back at square one, building the old bog-standard nest. Nothing changes until there's some random mutation in our genes, which can take generations, and the birds which have it turn out, by chance, to be better survivors than those without. It's the basic Darwinian theory of evolution by natural selection.'

Tom leant forward in his chair. 'I'm not a scientist, nor a doctor, but from what I'm told, the dogma that DNA and genes are the "blueprint of life", the sole, unalterable mechanism of inheritance is starting to be challenged. After they first unravelled the structure of DNA in the 1950s, they thought it was the answer to everything. When they started the human genome project in 1990, they expected to find 100,000 genes, but they ended up with only 24,000. That's about the same as a worm. Some are now suggesting the number is actually nearer 19,000. People are struggling to see how so few genes can account for the complexity of human life. There has to be something else involved. My friend says that there is general agreement among leading genetic researchers that they aren't yet smart enough even to realise what they don't know.'

Tom could sense that Dr Jacobson was starting to become irritated and tried to adopt a less lecturing tone. 'I know I sound like I'm just regurgitating numbers and statistics, but there is some real doubt out there. There have been several scientific studies that show that changes to a parent can be passed down to its offspring. You probably know about the agouti mouse experiment?'

'It rings a bell. I think it was in the Lancet, but there's so much in there, one has to concentrate on one's own field.'

Tom tried to look understanding before pressing on with his argument. 'I can well appreciate that. In this experiment, they changed the diet of some pregnant mice and it altered the shape and colour of their offspring. They went from being fat and blonde to thin and brown. Those are characteristics controlled by a specific gene, the so-called agouti gene. The point is, they didn't alter the diet of the children yet the new traits carried on through three or more generations before it faded. It was a reversible inherited change, passed down without any alteration to the DNA sequence of the mice. They call it epigenetics, the temporary chemical modification of DNA.'

The word epigenetics brought a smile of recognition to the doctor's face. 'There's a lot of hype about that at the moment. My understanding of its real role is as a mechanism for explaining how an individual animal's cells, which all form from a single fertilised egg and share exactly the same DNA, can become specialised. By causing certain genes to be activated and others suppressed, one cell becomes a liver cell, another becomes a brain cell.'

Tom nodded. 'That's right and I think that aspect of epigenetics is pretty non-controversial. The thing that seems to get people worked up is the role for epigenetics in inheritance. Let me just tell you about one more study and then I'll shut up.'

Tom took the doctor's silence as approval and carried on. 'They conditioned some laboratory mice to associate an electric shock with a particular odour. The mice then exhibited a fear response whenever they were exposed to that smell, even without the shock. There's an obvious parallel with the Pavlov's dog experiment, but the thing that was new was that the fear response was passed down to at least two further generations of mice. It was an inherited memory in the children and grandchildren of the mice who had actually received the shock. The mice were bred by IVF and never met their parents, so it had to be carried over through inheritance. You can see the evolutionary driver behind it, animals learning from their antecedents' experiences in order to adapt more quickly to changing environments. The details of actual event itself don't have to be consciously remembered, just the outcome.'

Doctor Jacobson held up a hand to signal that his patient should stop. 'Okay, Tom, I've let you talk through your argument. If I'm honest, I don't particularly enjoy being lectured on genetics by a layman. However, I can see you've been doing your research, though I suspect it's been rather selective. Let's say I accept that memories, in some primitive form, can be inherited. To go from a simple fear response, or slotting twigs together to form a nest, to seeing detailed events from your grandfather's past is like an archaeologist finding a single fragment of pot and building an entire culture.' Jacobson smiled. 'Some of them like to do that, of course, but it's not science. Look, I beseech you to give up on this. It really doesn't stand up to any kind of detailed scrutiny. You know that, I'm sure. Now, let's get back to reality. We need to discuss how to progress. You're off the Trempatolam now, so we need to move you onto something else. Just to calm you down. Maybe help with these slightly obsessional thoughts of yours.'

'No, thank you, doctor, but I don't want to take any more pills. I've given it a lot of thought and I've made my mind up. 100%.'

Jacobson shifted in his chair. He searched for signs of flexibility in Tom's eyes, and finding only resolve, decided to bring the consultation to a close.

'Well, I want you to understand you're going against my advice. I don't think you're a danger to yourself or others, so I can't insist you take medication. As for the inherited memories, you're not my only patient who chooses to believe in things I can't accept myself. Just try to relax about it. As time passes and your experiences with Trempatolam get more distant, I'm sure you'll find that easier. And talk to your sister. Maybe she'll have more success convincing you of the...' He paused as he searched for an appropriate word. '...improbability of what you are suggesting.'

He fixed Tom with a unsympathetic stare. 'I don't think there's any value in scheduling another appointment together at this stage. Should you have any concerns or anxieties in the future you can always contact Mrs Farrell and come back to see me.'

The doctor stood and gestured Tom towards the door.

Chapter twenty-nine

When Tom got back home he slumped down heavily on his sofa and threw his keys onto the coffee table. They skidded off and onto the carpet. He left them there. He sat back and wondered what he'd achieved in his session at the clinic. He hadn't convinced Dr Jacobson and he'd never expected to. He hadn't convinced Dave Dunstan either, though his friend had been a little more open-minded. Tom wasn't sure himself that epigenetics held the key, but at least it demonstrated that the deeper scientists looked, the more complex the model of inheritance became.

He picked up his laptop and stroked the touchpad to bring it back to life. He'd left it logged on and it displayed the web page he'd been reading earlier in the day. The page was from a popular science site and it reported the study of mice who had inherited the conditioned fear of a certain odour. The article ended with a quote from a leading geneticist saying there was 'a growing list of convincing models that question our previous assumptions and doctrine. These models tell us that something – we don't know what, as yet – but something is going on.'

Tom knew his dreams of his grandfather's life would always be treated with understandable suspicion by Jacobson, as would the similar accounts on the Trempatolam forum. Perhaps some of those reports were copycat stories from unreliable, drug-affected sources. But Tom knew he hadn't copied anyone, nor had at least one of the contributors on the forum.

'Something is going on' said Tom out loud. He knew it wasn't time travel. That would be the stuff of fantasy. If he'd appeared to influence historic events in any way, that was surely his subconscious mind superimposing his own inclinations and responses onto his grandfather's memories. More than ever, though, he was sure the essence of the events had occurred and were somehow locked in his mind.

He realised he needed to send an update email to his sister. He decided to focus on his efforts at job hunting, though he would have to mention his appointment at the clinic. He knew she would be concerned, angry even, that he'd refused alternative medication. He would placate her by telling her he felt fine, which he did, but he would avoid going into detail about his discussions with Dr Jacobson. Tom knew it was a lie by omission but it was a white lie for the sake of her feelings, and he promised himself that he would come clean when she was more confident of his health and stability.

He opened his email account to find three new messages in his inbox. The first was a list of current vacancies that loosely fitted his profile on one of the employment websites. The second was a brief note saying he had not been selected to go through to the next phase of recruitment for the 'outgoing personality' role. The third was from JaneJust, the contact for the family tree he'd found on the Web.

Dear Tom

I'm sorry I didn't reply sooner, but I've been away on a brief holiday and I'm one of those old fashioned people who likes to have a break from modern technology.
But how exciting to get an email from a (distant?) cousin! That's the benefit of putting your family tree online, I guess. My mother started the research years ago when my dad was still alive. I got involved more recently to help her with the Internet side of things, but it was her idea to upload it so that others could see it too. Sadly, she passed away last year, but I know she'd be <u>so</u> pleased that you'd got in touch.

I ought to explain where I fit on the tree. I'm 'living Evans', the widow of Anthony Evans. I'm the one with the four older brothers. I was something of a late afterthought - my parents were getting on a bit by the time I arrived, but I think they'd always wanted a girl and my brothers spoilt me rotten! My mother still shows as living Barrowclough (my maiden name, obviously). I haven't had the heart to update that even though she's no longer with us. Mum's maiden name was Hargreaves.

In your email you said your father was Thomas Haworth's son. The link between us is that Thomas Haworth's first wife was my mother's aunt, Clara. Mum never met her, but she had a photo of Clara and was always telling me how much I looked like her. Funny how things can skip a generation. Mum and I looked quite different.

My husband and I met at art college in Manchester and lived there for years. When he died I moved back home to Blackburn - property's so much cheaper - and of course, I could be with Mum. I used to work part time in an art gallery in Manchester, but now I've got a full time job at a charity based in your home town of Burnley. The money's better than the gallery but not great. At least it feels like I'm doing something worthwhile rather than flogging overpriced rubbish to people who wouldn't know a Mondrian from a colour chart.

How long is it since you moved up to London and do you ever get back up north? Next time you do, it would be really nice to meet.

With love
Jane x
PS How well did you know your grandfather, Thomas Haworth? Mum and I found out that he married two more times, and I realise you'd have been quite young when he died. Mum met him when she was a young child, but the family seemed to drift apart and I'd be interested to know more about him.

Tom could feel his heart beating in his chest. He read and reread one line of the email - *Mum never met her, but she had a photo of Clara.* His hands were shaking as he typed a response.

Dear Jane

Thanks for coming back to me. I've been in Burnley a couple of times recently. It's a shame we didn't get in touch with each other earlier. I'd really like to meet you too, but I don't know when I'll be up there again.

Last time, I went up with my sister Sarah. She lives in America now and I guess she would fit on your tree as 'Living Larsson'. She's married to Jim and they have two kids, Josh and Janey. They're all lovely. It's a pity I can't see them more often. They're the only family I've got left, I'm afraid.

Anyway, Sarah and I found Clara's grave. We didn't know she existed until very recently. You said your mother had a photo of her? I've never seen one. I guess when a man remarries his new wife doesn't want to be reminded of her predecessor. My sister's got all the family albums and Clara's not in there. Do you have the photo now? If so, I'd very much like to see it. I hope it's not an imposition, but would you be able to scan it?

I'm not sure what I can tell you about my grandfather. As you mentioned, he died when I was quite young. I've attached a picture of his third and final wedding. I'm the little lad in the suit. I'm not quite that cute anymore...

Thanks
Tom
PS I'd be really grateful if you were able to scan that photo of Clara.

Dear Tom

I'm dashing out, so this is just a quick message.

Thank you <u>so</u> much for the wedding photo you attached. It meant a lot to me to see your grandfather's face, albeit later in life. As I said, my mum met him when she was a child (and he was much younger), but she never had a picture of him.

I do have her photo of Clara. It's one of my treasures. I've got a hectic day at work tomorrow, but I'll try to get it scanned in and then I'll email it on to you.

I know what it's like when you're researching someone from your family's past. You find a name, when they were born, married and died, but it's kind of empty without a picture. When you see their face they become real.

Love
Jane xx
PS I'd really like to find out what you do remember about your grandfather, when you have the time.

Tom slept even more badly than usual. The prospect of some hard evidence was making him question any confidence he might have had. He kept turning over and over in his head the implications of seeing Clara's face, her real face, not the image in his mind. He could envisage three options. One, the photo was indistinct, blurred or faded. Clearly, that would tell him nothing. Two, it looked nothing like the Clara in his head. Would that mean everything he had started to believe was nonsense? Or was it possible his mind had overlaid a face onto an otherwise accurate recollection? Clara looked so like Amanda after all. It was possible, but he knew it would totally shatter any faith he had in the veracity of his dreams.

The third option was arguably the most disturbing. The photograph would be of his Clara. She came first. He would have been drawn to Amanda because of her resemblance to a woman hidden in the furthest reaches of his subconscious. If the photograph was of his Clara, he wasn't sure how he would cope. It was one thing having a crazy fantasy about remembering parts of someone else's life. It was quite another having proof, even if no-one could really see it but you.

He spent the next morning checking his inbox every few minutes. He tried to occupy his mind looking at job websites, but his eyes scanned across their words as if they were meaningless and impenetrable.

At 11:05 a new email finally arrived. It was from Jane, but not her personal JaneJust address, rather a work address starting jane_evans@. Tom prepared himself by forcing into his mind a picture of the Clara from his dreams. He felt his heart rate begin to accelerate and he stared at his inbox for a full two minutes before he had the courage to open the email. It had no message just a paper clip symbolising an attached photograph. He could tell it had been scanned at a very high resolution as the file size was unhelpfully large for a slow Internet connection such as his own. Tom clicked on the icon and lines of pixels began creeping down the white page as the image slowly emerged.

It was a monochrome with hints of sepia. The crown of the head appeared first. The hair was straight and the shade of grey suggested the mousy brown Tom wanted to see. Then came the forehead, then the eyes, the nose, the mouth, the chin. Tom sat back as the full face was revealed.

It was a passably attractive woman in her mid twenties. She had kind eyes that could have been mid brown. Tom looked more closely in case he was, somehow, mistaken. There was no mistake. It was not Clara.

Chapter thirty

Tom told himself that this was what he had expected. He tried to reason with his emotions. He failed. He found himself sinking into a quagmire of despair. It consumed him like bereavement, but it was a loss of absolute totality. Someone whose grave he had already visited had been taken from him completely. She had been purged from eternity. Not only was she dead, she had never existed. There was nothing of the Clara he knew. The ghostly memory he had clung to was a self-deceiving lie. Dr Jacobson was right.

For first time in weeks, Tom needed a drink. He'd got through sleepless nights and days of anxious confusion, but he couldn't cope with this. His thirst wasn't a distant, nagging longing anymore; it was an immediate, irresistible demand. His oath of abstinence felt worthless. Even when he'd repeated it in the graveyard he was deluding himself. He'd said he was giving it to a stranger in honour of his grandfather's love for her, not his own. It simply wasn't true. All along, he'd believed in her. And now she was gone.

He tried to call Dave. There was no reply, and despite leaving a garbled message, Tom decided he couldn't wait for the call to be returned. He knew the late morning clientele at the Duke of York were a seedy bunch; he'd joined their silent company often enough in the past. They would have to do. He grabbed his wallet and keys and slammed the flat door behind him

He slipped his key in the door and let himself back in. It was just before 6:00 pm. He was sober. He'd stood outside the pub and from somewhere found the strength to start walking away. He'd decided this was not the day to give up on himself. He'd carried on to the sanctuary of the library. This time he didn't use the computers to search out names from his past. He just sat quietly in the light airy rooms, an unopened newspaper on his lap, and come to terms with his loss. The more he thought, the more he realised there had never been anything to lose. He had been using a silly fantasy as a crutch. What he needed was real people, real friends, and a living, breathing replacement for Amanda, the wife he should finally accept was never coming back to him.

When he was back home in his living room, he sat down and checked his emails out of habit. There was another from jane_evans@. The subject line read: *If you want something doing.* He briefly considered what it could mean and opened the message.

Dear Tom

I need to apologise. As I said, I knew I was going to be busy today so I asked our Way to Work girl to scan in that picture for me. I don't know what they teach children at school these days. They seem to think as long as they make some kind of effort, it doesn't matter whether they get things right or wrong. And they never consider asking if they're not sure. I think they just want to get things out of the way so they can go back to texting their mates. That's probably not fair. She's a nice enough kid, but she lost the place in the album. So she found a photograph that 'looked the same' to her and scanned that. She doesn't have her own work email account, so I'd left mine logged on and she sent it from there. It was only when I checked my sent box this afternoon that I saw what she'd done. I guess it's not the end of the world. It's just a picture of a rather ordinary looking woman whom you never met after all. Anyway, here's the right one. If you want something doing, do it yourself...

Love
Jane xx

PS I suspect I'm in danger of sounding like a cracked record, but I am interested in what you know about your grandfather, however small it is.

There was another paper clip attached to the email. Tom's pulse began to race once again. This time his mood was tainted with resentment. He'd won this fight. It was over, sorted. His opponent had been down and out, but he'd just climbed back up from the floor of the ring. Tom would have to go yet another round.

The image file was much smaller this time and opened quickly. Tom's emotions were already shredded; he looked into the woman's face and tears of relief began to team down his own.

Chapter thirty-one

The doorbell rang. Tom's doorbell never rang, certainly not in the early evening. He rushed into the bathroom, splashed some water onto his face and then towelled it dry. In the mirror his eyes still looked red but they would have to do.

He went into the hall and saw the outline of a woman's head in the frosted glass that filled the upper half of his front door. He opened it and his wife was standing there. He hadn't seen her for months.

'Amanda, this is a surprise. Wow, you look really well.'

Her hair was much blonder than when he last saw it, and she had a healthy tan. Tom knew she burnt badly in the sun so presumed it was out of a bottle. All the same, it suited her. Her clothes looked expensive and he'd never seen her so attractive. Old feelings began to stir within him, but he quickly suppressed them. Over her shoulder, he could see a sports car parked in the street in front of the flat. He couldn't believe it belonged to any of his neighbours.

'Is that your Porsche?' he asked her.

She twisted her head to look at the car, then turned back to answer. 'Yes, it's only a Caymen, not a 911, but it's great fun. Are you driving anything at the moment?'

Tom shook his head. 'The occasional hire car. That's about it.'

Her eyebrows furrowed slightly when she saw the reddening round his eyes.

'You don't really need a car in London do you, Tom? Well, aren't you going to ask me in? I know I didn't ring ahead, but I can't imagine the place is an embarrassing tip. We both know how tidy you are.'

Tom couldn't tell if the comment was compliment or criticism. He gestured her in and then showed her into the living room. She sat on the sofa; he perched on the hard wooden bench built underneath the small bay window.

He couldn't think of a polite way of asking her why she was there. Fortunately, she resumed the conversation.

'Are you okay? You almost look like you've been crying.'

'No, don't be silly. It's hay fever or something.'

'Mmm. I saw Jimmy the other day, Jimmy Mills that is. He said you'd resigned, that there'd been some sort of trouble in the office. Are you still drinking, Tom? I had to call in some favours to get you that job. You're on your own this time, my boy.'

Tom felt like asking what sort of favours, but he resisted.

'You know I was grateful for you getting me the job, Mand, but I was like a fish out of water. I didn't fit in there. I'm off the booze, honest. I'm applying for various things, jobs I'm more suited to. I'm quietly confident it's all going to work out well.'

Amanda nodded, but her eyes suggested disbelief, or perhaps it was just disinterest. She got the discussion back on track.

'I'm sure you're wondering why I've called round. I won't waste your time with pleasantries. I'm in a relationship—'

'With Jimmy?'

'No, not with Jimmy! He's got a wife for God's sake! It's with someone at work. It's getting quite serious, and I think it's about time you and I sorted things out between ourselves. Wrap up our marriage so we can both move on.'

'Divorce you mean? I thought we had to be separated for two years?'

'It's easier if you've been apart for two years, but we'll just use your unreasonable behaviour as grounds. It'll be straightforward; I work for a law firm, don't forget. I'll sort it all out. And needless to say, I'm not expecting anything from you financially. Well, it wouldn't do me much good if I were. Sorry, that's a bit below the belt. I'm also assuming you don't expect to get anything from me. We've already sorted out the house. We caught the market at just the right time, by the way. I knew I was right to listen to my contacts in the property business. I'll just need you to sign a few forms for the divorce, and that's it, we're history.'

Tom looked at the woman he'd once loved and raised his hands in a gesture of compliant surrender.

'History it is.'

Amanda said goodbye on the doorstep, and Tom found himself awkwardly offering to shake to her hand. She looked at him dismissively before they both turned to see Dave Dunstan waving a greeting as he padded down the street towards them.

He rushed up to them and tried to give Amanda a kiss on the cheek. She recoiled, partly because of his unwanted invasion into her personal space but also from the stale alcohol fumes on his breath. Undeterred, he babbled at her enthusiastically.

'Amanda, it's good to see you! You're looking really well, Sheila! I might go as far as to say you're looking fair dinkum, in fact.'

'Oh, for God sake! Haven't you grown out of that yet?' she sighed, quietly but audibly. She turned once more to Tom and looked at him accusingly.

'You two going down the pub, I suppose? So much for being off the booze, eh? Still, not my problem any more. Goodbye, Tom. I'll be in contact by email.'

The two men silently watched her as she strode over to the Porsche, lowered herself in and then roared off down the street.

'I'm still not her favourite person, I see' said Dave.

'Nor am I, mate. Nor am I.'

Tom paused thoughtfully and then put his hand on his friend's shoulder. 'Dave, what are you doing on this side of town?'

'You sounded really stressed out in the phone message you left me, cobber. I tried to call you back several times, but you didn't pick up. I thought I'd better do a walkabout over this way and check you were okay.'

'Oh look Dave, I'm so sorry! This is the second time this has happened. I really must start carrying that bloody mobile phone around with me. At least you haven't flown over from America, I suppose. Oh God! All I can do is apologise. You're a good mate and I'm an idiot. Please come in.'

After confirming he had nothing stronger in the flat, Tom made tea for them both and they sank down next to each other on the sofa.

'All she's done is bring forward the inevitable. You never actually thought you were going to get back together did you, cobber?' asked Dave.

'No, of course not. Well, maybe. But look, something else has happened that's a distraction, to say the least.'

'The photo you mentioned in your phone message? Don't you think it's for the best? You didn't really expect to recognise her? I mean, it was just a silly fantasy. At least you can stop fretting about it now.'

'No, Dave, you don't understand. I got a second email, a correction. Look, I'll show you.'

Tom opened the laptop and brought up the scanned photograph. Dave lifted up his glasses and began to nod as he squinted at the screen. 'Well, she definitely has a passing resemblance to Amanda.'

'More importantly, she is the woman I saw in those dreams.'

'Those drink and drug induced dreams?'

'Dave, I'm stone cold sober now and that is the face I was expecting to see before I opened the email.'

'You're sure it's not just wishful thinking? You're not talking yourself into this because you're so desperate for it to be true?'

'No. I know I can't prove it to you, but you'll have to take my word for it.'

'Okay, cobber, let's say it is the woman you dreamt about. The rational explanation is that you must have seen a picture of her before. It was buried somewhere in that memory of yours.'

'My sister's got all the family photo albums. She said there was no-one in them that looked anything like Amanda.'

'Mmm. That doesn't sound what you'd call conclusive. And anyway, maybe your grandfather kept a photo of his first wife somewhere separate. He might have got it out to show you before he died. Old men get sentimental and reflective. You never know, he might have asked to be buried with it. That could be why it's not in the albums.'

Tom's brow furrowed at his friend's logic. He stuttered a reply. 'But... but... Why would it make such an impact on me? Why would I spend my life looking for a woman who resembled her? It looks like Amanda, but it also looks a bit like Christine. Remember her?'

Dave nodded again. 'Now Christine was a nice girl. You should have married her. Bigger koalas than Amanda, that's for... Sorry, mate. I know this is serious for you. I must stop being infantile.'

He looked again at the scanned image on the laptop and it prompted a question. 'Remind me who sent you the photo. Jane, you said?'

'She's descended from Clara's family, the Hargreaves. Hang about, I printed off the family tree when I was in the library. I've got it somewhere.'

Tom had carefully filed the printout and found it quickly.

'Yeh, here she is. She's the granddaughter of Clara's brother Harold and his wife Mary.' Tom hesitated as he studied that section of the document closely for the first time.

'That's odd' he said.

Chapter thirty-two

Dear Jane

Many thanks for emailing the photo. I'm sorry it caused you so much trouble. You said it was just picture of an ordinary looking woman whom I never met, but I recognised her. I've had these dreams - forgive me if this seems a little barmy - and it was her face that was in those dreams. My friend tells me that the only rational explanation is that I must have seen the picture before, and perhaps he's right. Perhaps my grandfather showed it to me when I was a child.

I'm sorry I haven't responded to your request for information about my grandfather. That's because I'm not sure what I do know about him anymore. What I know for certain is that he died when I was too young to really remember him. I think I can recall his wedding to the woman I knew as Grandma, but I grew up seeing the photo I sent you and I suspect my memories are based on that. I've done some family history research about him recently, but I don't think I've uncovered any names or information that you hadn't already found and included in your own family tree. My sister recalls our mother saying that our grandfather's second wife - my dad's mother - was a 'right bitch' who fell out with all my grandfather's relations, but I'm not sure that would stand up as evidence in a court of law.

I did have a question about your family tree. Clara's brother, Harold, and his wife, Mary, had one child, your mother. I wasn't surprised when I saw she was an only child because I understood Mary had lost one baby and was told she would have difficulty conceiving again. It's only when I looked at the tree again that I noticed your mother's date of birth, in April 1929. Are you sure that year is correct or has it been typed in wrongly? Forgive me if I don't explain why I'm questioning the date - you really will think I'm barmy - but it is important to me to know for sure.

Thanks again for the photo and I hope we are able to meet up sometime soon.

Tom

Tom pressed the send button and hoped Jane wouldn't be concerned by the mention of his dreams or his questioning her mother's date of birth. He tried to put it out of his mind and began to concentrate on how to word a second email. It was time for him to be more honest with his sister. He owed it to her, and somehow he had to do it without distressing her too much.

Chapter thirty-three

Dear Tommy

Greetings from Minnesota. Jim, Josh, Janey and I are all fine.

Thanks for the update. There was a lot for you to talk about this time. I know it doesn't come naturally for you to send such regular emails, but hearing from you stops me fretting - even if what you have to tell me is rather worrying.

Wow. A royal visit from Amanda and she's blonde as well as skinny now? That's a treat for the world. Seriously, though, you must have known divorce was inevitable once you'd sold the house. I suspect you're putting on a brave face, but now you can forget about her, and dare I say it, concentrate on finding someone else. How about a nice, down to earth, northern girl? A <u>real</u> one and perhaps one who isn't bordering on anorexic? (Also, while I'm slagging off Amanda, there's something really common about driving a Porsche, don't you think?)

And now to the thornier part of your last email. I was beginning to suspect you hadn't really put this to bed. It's alright you saying you're fine and in control and that I shouldn't be concerned. How am I supposed to feel when you resurrect this mad idea of living out events in our grandfather's life? I guess this theory about inherited memories is vaguely plausible - I must admit I've always been a little intrigued by stories of previous lives and reincarnation - but please don't get obsessed by it. It's good you're seeing Dave again, so long as you don't let him lead you astray. His heart was always in the right place, and it sounds like he's trying to keep you grounded. His suggestion of double checking that Clara's photo definitely isn't in the family albums was a good one. Like him, I was hoping I'd find it. I'm tempted to tell you it is there, but I'm not going to lie, it's not. And yes, Clara does look like Amanda and, to an extent, Christine too. (Now, Christine was a nice girl. You never know, she might be single again - you could try to find her on facebook?)

Jane sounds interesting. I hope she resolves your mysterious 'anomaly', though maybe I shouldn't? From what you said, she is single and also, of course, northern. I'm betting she has a healthy, robust figure as well. (Oops, another dig at Amanda.)

Oh, Tommy! Look after yourself, stay sober and please don't make yourself ill again by getting too worked up by this photo business. Like Dave, I'm sure there's a simple, rational explanation. Please try to prepare yourself for when you find it.

Keep keeping in touch.
Love Sarah xxx

Hi Tom

Sorry for not replying sooner. Your email came as a bit of a shock and it's taken me a couple of days to get my thoughts together. To be honest, I felt betrayed by my husband when he died – that's a story for another day - and perhaps I find it difficult to trust men now. That's silly - you're family after all - and I don't think you're out to trick me. That said, there are some things in your email, some things you seem to know, that I really don't understand.

You're right about the anomaly in the family tree. My mother wanted it to stay secret because she thought some kind of crime had been committed. Even if it was, it wasn't hers and all those involved are dead now, so I don't think I need to keep hiding it, at least not from you.

Harold and Mary Hargreaves, the couple who raised my mother, the people on her birth certificate, were not her biological parents. It was a different time back then. Before computers it was easier to hide information, and the family also relocated from Rossendale to Blackburn at about the same time. That may have been a deliberate effort to cover their tracks, or maybe they were already in the process of moving because Harold had got a job there. I can't be sure.

Harold and Mary had very recently lost their own baby and then, as I think you know, Harold's sister Clara died in childbirth. It was a matter of days later. Your grandfather, our grandfather, obviously thought the best thing for his baby, my mother, was for her to be raised by close family. Adoption had always been an informal arrangement until it was given legal status in a 1926 Act of Parliament. My mother was born only three years later and so the new process of getting court approval probably seemed very complex and alien. Harold simply recorded the birth in a different registration district and then, as far as officialdom was concerned, he and his wife had a new baby daughter. You wouldn't get away with it today, but as I said, they were different times. And if it was a crime, I struggle to see who the victim was. Perhaps it was my mother. She lived in ignorance of the deception until her widowed father was almost on his deathbed. My mother was shocked, but she'd had a very happy childhood with warm and loving parents who were unable to have any more children themselves. Perhaps the victim was our grandfather. He gave away his daughter and eventually they became estranged.

Maybe he didn't want to risk exposing the lie or maybe there was something else that caused him to drift out of her life. It was interesting that your mother said his second wife, Ann, caused a rift in the family. That could explain a lot.

You'll understand now why I was so interested in your grandfather, but there is another reason which is a bit weirder, if I'm honest. I've not spoken about this for years and back then I only told my husband. I'm only telling you because of what you said about recognising Clara's face from a dream.

When Tony and I were at art college, he considered himself a wild bohemian. He'd take any drugs that were going and he dragged me down the same path. There was one pill that really messed up my head. I had these crazy dream-like trips and saw myself as a young woman in the early part of last century. At first they were set in Rossendale – where our families come from - then they moved down to Burnley. There was even a Wakes Week holiday in Blackpool. There were a few episodes, mostly happy, but ultimately the experience nearly drove me mad. I've been clean ever since. I'm not even keen on drinking alcohol. I'd pretty much forgotten about it until

Mum told me her guilty secret. She showed me that photo of Clara, my grandmother. It's been years and my memory's probably playing tricks, but she was the woman I saw when I was taking the drug. I'm almost sure of it. Or maybe I am finally going mad.

There you go, I've told you everything. Somehow I think I can trust you. I hope I'm right. For the sake of my mother's memory, please don't broadcast the fact that her birth record was fraudulent. I certainly don't intend correcting the online family tree, though obviously I'm happy for you to tell your sister.

Love Jane xx

Dear Jane

Thank you for your email and your openness. I'm sorry there were things in my previous email that you didn't understand. I'd rather explain face to face and I really would like to see you. I'm between jobs at the moment (you don't know anyone looking for an unemployed statistician do you?) so I can come up to Blackburn or Burnley anytime. It would give me a break from filling in application forms and reading rejection letters. Please let me know when would be convenient. I could get on a train first thing tomorrow morning, or the next day, or whenever. Just tell me what works for you.

Jane, I really need to see you as soon as possible. I hope this email doesn't come across as strange and that you still want to meet me.

Love Tom

Chapter thirty-four

As the train glided north, Tom leaned his head against the window and watched the scenery flick by. He saw the familiar Norman castle close by the tracks but somehow missed the mysterious churchyard mounds. He wondered if he had been mistaken. Perhaps they belonged to a different train, on a different line. His mind kept returning to other images from his past. It was all his past now, part of what made him who he was, whether he lived it or someone else. In one sense, he believed he had lived through the memories he inherited from his grandfather: the two men shared a quarter of their genetic make-up, so there was always something of Tom there. Perhaps he showed through at times, like when the normally hard-bitten corporal showed kindness and concern for the frightened boy soldier in that ghastly trench.

His thoughts switched to Jane and her drug-induced dreams. He wasn't aware Trempatolam had ever been adopted by those looking for a recreational high, and it wouldn't have been available when she was at college anyway. A different pill must have had a similar psychoactive effect. He wondered if the exaggerated stories of past life regression so derided by Dr Jacobson had always been rooted in genuine cases of unlocked memories, whether released by drugs or some other mechanism. Tom briefly considered whether hypnosis could take him back to Clara once more. He dismissed the idea. He had to live his life in the here and now, not vicariously in the past of another man.

As for Jane, he recognised that she would have difficulty accepting that he, too, had seen actual events from Clara's past. Who wouldn't? He knew he would have to tell his story carefully to avoid appearing like a deluded copycat, or worse, a sly trickster.

He'd arranged to meet her at 2:00 pm in the cafe in the market square. She was taking the afternoon off as she'd been working extra hours and the charity preferred to give time off in lieu rather than pay overtime. She was attending a colleague's lunchtime leaving drink first and would then spend the rest of the day with her new-found cousin.

Tom was anxious about the meeting, and given the potential delays inherent in long distance travel, had wanted to arrive as early as he could. The local train pulled into the station just after noon, and he found himself with nearly two hours to kill. The skies had brightened after the drizzle of central England, so he decided to take a circuitous walk via the canal. Burnley had been built on the flat valley floor at the confluence of the rivers Brun and Calder. The railway viaduct spanned the gap between the hills and the canal from Liverpool entered the town clinging to the side of the valley opposite the station. Tom's route took him down from the depressing derelict buildings by the train line, through a characterless modern retail park and then past the shells of old mills and warehouses until he climbed back up a steep incline to the canal. He'd reached the area christened the Weavers' Triangle by those intent on preserving the town's industrial heritage, and a fine new open square and refurbished canalside terraces spoke at last of investment and hope. The sun reflected off the faintly rippling water onto fresh stonework which glowed honey yellow and golden cream. Tom felt the warmth of renewed affection for an old friend. He continued along the contour hugging towpath until the waterway turned sharply to the left and shot arrow-straight across the valley on a 60 foot high embankment known as the

Straight Mile. This one-time engineering wonder let him look out over his home town and pick out the old from the new, finding the buildings and sights he remembered from his childhood and, he sensed, before. After walking halfway along, he reached steps that led down into the central market area, long since pedestrianised. Before he descended, he looked back over his shoulder towards the familiar sweep of high moors that walled the town. Almost dead-centre, on the crown of the tallest hill, he saw an indistinct black shape that could have been a lone tree. He realised it was, albeit a tree of iron that sang in the wind. The skies had begun to cloud over, and the drizzle he had left behind in the Midlands caught up with him. He hurried down the steps and decided to head towards the covered market hall for shelter. Once again, he found himself passing the Hop Inn and he hesitated outside its door. He was starting to get wet; it was lunchtime, and the pub did serve food, of sorts. He decided he should have a snack; he assumed Jane would have already eaten by the time they met. The last time he'd entered this pub, his teetotal resolve had failed. He knew he was stronger now.

He walked through the door and went straight towards the bar. The same barmaid was standing there, idly checking her nails. She greeted Tom with a smile that had warmth but lacked recognition. This time, Tom asked for a Coke. Glass in hand, he picked up a menu and then turned to survey the pub and its clientele. Not surprisingly, little had changed since his last visit. The decorators had still not been summoned, and the blue-topped pool table was still there, though it now supported a handwritten sign saying 'out of order'.

In the shadowy corner where Tom had imagined he'd seen his youthful father was a cluster of people in hushed conversation. Occasionally, one or other of them would look over their shoulder at a nearby table where a woman sat with a large, shaven-headed man. The man was leaning towards the woman, talking animatedly and sometimes reaching out to try to touch her arm. Her body language suggested she was uncomfortable with his advances: she was sitting back in her chair with her torso twisted slightly away from him and her arms folded across her chest. She looked up, saw Tom and began waving towards him.

Tom realised he recognised her. It was Amanda.

He stared incredulously as his eyes adjusted to the dim light. Her hair had gone back to a darker shade, but it was unmistakably… No, it wasn't Amanda. It was someone else he knew. It was Clara.

She was still waving. Tom walked over slowly. The large man saw him coming and glowered threateningly. The woman spoke first.

'Tom? You're early. How did you know I'd be in here?'

'Jane? It is Jane, isn't it? You look so like her. It's… well, you look so like her.'

She smiled appreciatively. 'I told you I did. A few more wrinkles now and the odd grey hair obviously—'

The large man interrupted. 'I happen to be talking to this lady, pal. Why don't you just fuck off?'

For the first time, Tom noticed the man's ugly collection of mismatched tattoos on arms made thick and powerful by years of manual labour. Nonetheless, Tom continued talking in an even tone.

'I'm her cousin. Half-cousin, actually. We didn't know each other existed until a day or so ago. I've just come up from London this morning to see her.'

'You're a fucking cockney, are you?' It was more accusation than question.

Tom shook his head. 'Nah, I'm a Burnley boy. Went down to London to work and ended up married. Now I've got no job and no wife. Maybe it's time I came back home. The old place is growing on me again.'

Tom smiled and offered his hand to the other man. 'I'm Tom, by the way.'

A look of acceptance replaced the aggression on the large man's face as he reluctantly shook hands. 'Yeh, nice to meet you, pal.' He took a swig from his beer and sighed defeatedly. 'Oh alright, I'll leave you and your cousin to catch up. I were getting nowhere with her anyway.'

He picked up his pint and went back towards the bar. Tom took his place at the table.

Jane leaned forward conspiratorially and whispered. 'I'm sorry for dragging you into that, but thank you for rescuing me. He was a bit scary wasn't he? By the smell of his breath, he'd been in here all morning. My so-called friends and colleagues all backed away when he came over. And I don't think my Tony would have been as calm and as brave as you.'

Tom shook his head. 'Courage isn't my forte. To be fair, I wasn't exactly being confrontational. He was very unlikely to thump me.'

Tom paused briefly while he scanned the wall behind Jane as if he expected a ghost to walk through it. He looked back at her and continued thoughtfully. 'My dad always said "Don't run away from things that probably won't happen." Actually, it was "Cheer up. It might never happen," but I think that's what he meant. It's not a philosophy I've always been able to adhere to in the past.'

Suddenly, there was some shouting at the bar. One of the other customers had been pushed off his stool onto the floor, and the barmaid was threatening the large tattooed man with the police unless he left. A glass was smashed into the floor and then the door kicked open as he stormed out.

'You can all fuck off! I don't want to drink in this shithole anyway!' was still ringing round the pub as the atmosphere slowly calmed.

Everyone had been staring, but Tom turned back fractionally before Jane. He caught her face in profile for the first time and saw the neat, straight line of her nose. It wasn't Clara's nose. He wondered if Jane knew. Perhaps all she had to go on was a single face-on photograph or, perhaps, a half-remembered image in a mirror.

She saw that he had been focussing on her face and looked back enquiringly.

He answered with a question of his own. 'How did you know it was me? When I was at the bar and you waved. You've seen a photo of me when I was four, but I think I've changed quite a lot since then.'

She smiled. 'This is going to sound silly, but... your face, I've seen it before. It's your grandfather's face, the face of the man in my dreams; the ones I told you about. The ones I had in my crazy student days.'

Tom rocked his head ruefully. 'I wish I could tell you I was just like him as a person, but I'm not. He and I are rather different, though perhaps less than I once thought.'

They sat and chatted happily and easily like they were long-lost friends, two people with a shared but distant past, finally reunited after a lifetime of experiences. They talked of their upbringings, their marriages, their challenges and their hopes. Tom eventually, and cautiously, began to describe his experiences with Trempatolam and his memories of his grandfather's life and, of course, of Clara. Jane rediscovered her previous wariness and stared into his eyes like a stone-faced poker player looking for a tell of truth or deceit.

They'd both been on soft drinks, but the rest of the leaving party had consumed several rounds of alcohol and were becoming lively and loud.

Some music came on the jukebox. Tom and Jane stayed seated, but the others moved over to the open area in front of the speakers and began to dance enthusiastically. The song was a favourite, up-tempo tune from the eighties and Tom had to raise his voice a notch to be heard above it.

'You know what, lass? I reckon we could one-step to this'.

Epilogue

Lines of matching gravestones sit in perfect symmetry amidst striped green grass and weedless beds of flowers whose colour and aroma bring warmth and life to the place of the dead. All is beauty, tranquillity and respect despite the passing of the years and the dimming of the memories.

The ancient gardener hoes the same soil he has worked for nearly sixty years. He knows all their names, their ranks, their regiments, their ages. His own uncles lie in another field in France, different but the same.

These men are from England. The gardener has never made the short journey across the channel. In his younger years he used an atlas to trace the homes of those whose graves he tends: soldiers of the Royal Sussex, the Durham Light Infantry, the Sherwood Foresters, and as here, the East Lancs. It is a geography he no longer remembers.

His mother was a superstitious countrywoman, and he was raised to believe the spirits of those who meet a violent end keep ghostly watch over those whose lives touched their own. Only when the last soul has found peace can they finally be at rest themselves.

Beneath the gardener's feet lie the partly disarticulated bones of a boy soldier. The flesh has fallen from his pure-white skull. The blight of red raw acne that once scarred the youthful face has long since faded away. Without sinew or muscle the jaw drops and gently twists.

The gardener cannot, will never, see that naked face. But if he did, he would surely see an expression written upon it. Alfred Langport is smiling.

56995613R00124

Made in the USA
Columbia, SC
03 May 2019